Your Golden Sun Still Shines

Your Golden Sun Still Shines

San Francisco: Personal Histories & Small Fictions

Denise Sullivan
editor

Manic D Press
San Francisco

ISBN 978-1-945655-05-9. For information, please address Manic D Press, PO Box 410804, San Francisco, California 94141 www.manicdpress.com
Printed in the USA
cover photo by Emily Beeson

Contents

Rename

Kim Shuck

In the radical renaming we will call homes
Five alarm fire we will call a
Hardware store the
Point of ignition we who will not move will be
Changed
Until we don't
Recognize until we can't
See for the smoke and the
Words that fire lifts from the walls
Written there by someone else and the
Names on the writhing flicker maps are a
Matchstick puzzle we can barely use to warm our hands

Lago de los Dolores

Alvin Orloff

Had it been around two centuries ago, the building where I live, in San Francisco's Mission District, would've been on the south bank of a small lake. Lago de los Dolores, the Lake of Sorrows, is long gone but were it still here I could travel downtown by ferry, water taxi, gondola, or perhaps in a tule reed canoe of the sort once produced by the native Ohlone people.

Water travel can be delightfully calming. The gentle rocking of the boat lulls one into a state of tranquility. Feel the fresh breeze on your face! Smell the briny water! See the gulls soaring and swooping! Hear the gentle roar of the sea! Shall we purchase a little something from the snack bar? I'm always up for salted peanuts. My, this ferry-boat sure is nicer than a Muni bus!

For reasons unrecorded (but surely related to rising property values), Lago de los Dolores was filled in during the middle years of the 19th century. When the 1906 earthquake hit, water rushed back in, liquefying the land. Buildings not only collapsed but sank

– including the first three stories of the Valencia Hotel, in which forty people drowned. You might not think of people drowning in an earthquake, but they do.

The name "Lake of Sorrows" always reminds me of Julie London singing the classic 1950s torch song, "Cry Me A River," composed by Arthur Hamilton. Others have sung it, but it will always be Julie's song.

Some historians insist Lago de los Dolores was not a lake, nor even a lagoon, but merely a stream, perhaps with a tidal inlet attached. They are quite certain the Valencia Hotel sank because of a broken water main and become peevish when disbelieved.

Local legend has it that reincarnated souls from the Lost Continent of Atlantis are especially attracted to San Francisco – possibly because the Transamerica Pyramid reminds them of their pyramid-strewn ancient homeland, now submerged below the ocean waves. This is said to account for San Francisco's widely noted civic predilections toward odd frolics and peculiar whimsies.

The first European to see Lago de los Dolores was Juan Bautista de Anza, a Basque explorer working for the Spanish crown. There is a commemorative plaque on Albion Street where it's thought that he, in March 1776, set up camp beside the lake.

A local paper recently printed an interview in which an Albion Street resident (a software engineer, if you're curious) called the plaque a "nuisance" because it attracts tourists and drunken teenagers. "It would be one thing if there were some historical building," he said, "but there's nothing here."

The aforementioned software engineer wants the commemorative plaque removed. Environmentalists have suggested restoring Lago de los Dolores. One can imagine a really big earthquake accomplishing both tasks simultaneously.

Of all the phrases one can utter, "there's nothing here" has got to be one of the saddest.

Anza discovered Lago de los Dolores while scouting locations for a presidio and Roman Catholic mission. The lake, back then, would have been surrounded by willow trees, waterfowl, reeds, mosquitos, and perhaps a few grizzly bears. Nearby sat the Ohlone villages of Chutchui and Sitlintac.

Soon after arriving, the Spanish founded the Mission Dolores, around which grew up a settlement they called "Yerba Buena." They conscripted (i.e., enslaved) the local Ohlone as agricultural laborers and expropriated (i.e., stole) their land, nearly wiping them out. In 1834, the Mexican government, which had succeeded the Spanish as rulers of California, ordered the Missions to turn over their property for redistribution. The Ohlone were supposed to get land grants but somehow most everything wound up in the hands of administrators and Mexican-owned rancherias.

I moved into my current building in 1989, just after the Loma Prieta earthquake. Across town sidewalks buckled, buildings tilted, and windows filled with "For Rent" signs. This last point surprised me: Who'd leave a glorious city like San Francisco just because of a little thing like a 6.9 magnitude earthquake?

The Ohlone practiced the Kuksu religion, which used rituals and narrative dances to supplicate for health, good harvests, fertility, and nice weather, as well as express mourning and commune with the spirit world. A secret society of Kuksu men held dances in underground vaults while wearing elaborate costumes and disguises. To me, such dances sound very San Francisco.

The Spanish also founded El Presidio Real de San Francisco, the Royal Fortress of Saint Francis, on the northern shore of their settlement. In the fictional future sci-fi universe of *Star Trek,* the

Presidio is headquarters for the United Federation of Planets, effectively making it the capital of the universe. I'll bet Anza didn't see *that* coming.

When I was growing up in the suburbs outside San Francisco, kids referred to the city as "SF" and called it a "freak magnet" due to the prevalence of odd frolics and peculiar whimsies. How long ago was that? If you were under 18 you could ride the Muni for a nickel, that's how long.

In 1848 California got manifest-destined into the US of A (via the Mexican-American war) and Yerba Buena, renamed San Francisco, quickly grew into a small city. The area where my building now stands – just past the outskirts of town – might have been an orchard, farmland, or perhaps used to graze livestock. Bird's-eye view landscape paintings from that era make the city and its environs look rather appealing.

On first arriving in San Francisco, I felt indifferent to the city's charms. Over the years, however, it gradually enchanted me with its quirky bookstores, snazzy Victorians, and funny old streetcars. I grew to love the ethnic diversity, the roiling fog, the absence of summer, the absence of winter, the absence of Republicans. Now, some forty years on, I have a nervous dread of being forced to live elsewhere.

During the late 19th century, the land over and around what had once been Lago de los Dolores, now simply referred to as "The Mission," became well known for vulgar amusements. One could go there to see dueling, bear fights, horse racing, baseball, or perhaps visit the famous Woodward's Gardens, which featured an amusement park, zoo, art gallery, and aquarium.

The last fluent speaker of an Ohlone language, the beautifully named Isabella Meadows, died in 1939.

If an earthquake doesn't recreate Lago de los Dolores, rising sea levels caused by global warming certainly could. To protect its landmass from the rising tides, San Francisco might need to build a series of dikes, as they've done in Holland. This would require a lot of pumping stations powered by windmills… which could be *hella* picturesque.

A defining characteristic of modern San Franciscans is our disinclination to judge fellow citizens based on their sexual habits or preferred methods of intoxication. About everything else, however, we are extra judge-y.

Constructed in 1880 as a hotel, the building in which I live is charmingly tilted and ramshackle. There's even a ghost inhabiting one of the closets: a small, quiet gentleman of late Victorian vintage. Sometimes, especially during the month of November, his shadow slips into the hallway, flickering lights, and giving people the creeps.

A few multinational corporations engaged in globe-spanning crimes of unspeakable evil are headquartered in San Francisco, but most San Franciscans would cheer their demise with unfeigned glee.

Following the 1906 earthquake, broken water mains rendered the city's fire hydrants useless just as dozens of gas fires erupted, incinerating thousands upon thousands of buildings. When the flames headed south it looked like the Mission was doomed, but then… a miracle! A working hydrant was discovered on 20th Street and its water halted the conflagration just a few yards north of the building in which I now live. Grateful citizens still gather annually to paint the miracle hydrant gold.

Even with dikes and windmills, it's likely that global warming's rising tides will eventually submerge low-lying San Francisco, reducing the city to a chain of tiny islands. Residents of drowned neighborhoods would need to relocate into underwater bubble buildings. Sightseeing attractions like the Mission Dolores would be visible only to scuba divers, and Muni would have to replace streetcars with submarines.

Ghosts are scary but I'm more frightened by the absence of ghosts. Un-haunted buildings lack soul.

The 20th century saw the Mission District lapse into quietude as a working-class residential neighborhood with lots of immigrants, first from the more downscale regions of Europe, later Latin America. Then, seduced by the cheap rent and delicious burritos, artists, eggheads, and oddballs began moving in. The area took on a pleasingly festive, bohemian atmosphere with a plethora of arty cafes, avant-garde galleries, open mics, and wild nightclubs.

If underwater bubble buildings prove impractical, as well they might, San Franciscans displaced by rising sea levels could move onto houseboats. Lots and lots of houseboats. An armada of houseboats. Everyone could reside on their own little craft and float to different island neighborhoods as their fancies dictate. When people married, they'd dock together. To divorce, they'd just pull anchor and sail in opposite directions. Quite practical, wouldn't you say?

The number of artists, oddballs, and eggheads living in the Mission has been dropping precipitously since the late 1990s due to rising rents, evictions, and a real estate frenzy caused by an influx of affluent tech workers. That the "techies" tend be more interested in pricey artisanal food and phone apps than odd frolics and peculiar whimsies is widely considered (among non-techies) to be an existential threat to San Francisco's civic culture.

From certain vantage points near my home, one can – in late afternoon – face west and behold a gigantic bank of fog looming over the city. As evening falls, the fog stretches, creeps, puffs, and mists down over the city, erasing streets, trees, and houses until all one sees is a mass of ghostly white oblivion.

The San Francisco Bay nearly met the same fate as Lago de los Dolores. People wanted to fill it in out of a misguided commitment to industry and progress. How tasteless can people be? Pretty darn tasteless.

My landlord recently announced plans to gut my building and replace it with a block of ultra-modern luxury units. Should the city grant him the permits (as they almost certainly will), my roommates and I could face permanent exile from San Francisco. What will become of our closet ghost? I have no idea.

Some claim Anza named Lago de los Dolores as such because he saw a few Ohlones standing by the shore, weeping. What were they sad about? Could they see into the future? Others believe the name was chosen because Anza first saw the lake on the Friday of Sorrows, a day Roman Catholics devote to the contemplation of the sorrowful Blessed Virgin Mary. There was nothing sad about the lake, except maybe that it was fated to disappear.

Should sea levels rise so much that every last inch of San Francisco is consigned to a watery grave, I hope our legend – like that of Atlantis – will live on. It would be nice to think of people a thousand years hence hearing tales of a beautiful foggy city with a genius for odd frolics and peculiar whimsies.

Hammering Nickels on Liberty Street

Sylvia J. Martinez

I grew up on Liberty Street in San Francisco's Mission District with a band of kids united by the number 14, the street address of the building where our single mothers rented apartments, each packing up her three kids and leaving a husband within five years of each other. The mothers didn't know one another when they moved in, but we kids smelled each other like a homeless person smells leftovers in a trashcan. Fresh! There were nine of us, ranging in ages around six to twelve, all born in the late '60s and early '70s. We matched up in age and grade almost perfectly. Our summertime playgroup met a minimum of eight hours a day, five days a week, sans parental chaperones. The minute we all heard the gentle slam signaling the last mom leaving for work, we'd all meet at the B's apartment.

Brianna, Betty, and Boris lived next door, which meant we literally shared a wall; our living room wall was their bedroom wall. Their mom Savannah, a tall and glamorous Filipina, had a suitor who knew that wooing her meant wooing her kids, too. He would bring them bags and bags of the kid-friendly food that taunted me during the commercials on my Saturday morning viewings of the *The Smurfs* and *Scooby Doo*. My own mom left my two older sisters and me cornflakes, bananas, and milk for breakfast, so instead we'd usually opt out and eat our morning meal at the B's instead. I was introduced to Pop-Tarts and Lucky Charms there, any child's fantasy breakfast. I think their mom's courtship with Mr. Wonka kept us from tantrums at the local market since we all got what we wanted next door. The B kids' gentleman caller must have either known he was feeding the stray kids or thought his beloved's babes had tapeworms since I remember there always being enough food for all of us.

After breakfast, we would play anything, anywhere. The older kids would flock upstairs to the Vega residence, where they had the only stereo system among the three families. Michael Jackson's *Off the Wall* album would permeate the walls of building 14, and the kids would bounce off them. "Life ain't so bad at all! Live your life off the wall!" The younger children would remain downstairs at our apartment, the Martinez kids' residence, or at the B's place playing dress-up or doctor or school or store with any materials we could find around the apartment. I can't remember how many toilet paper casts were carefully put on my leg or arm. Come to think of it, it was good practice for the two fractures I would endure a few years down the road while playing schoolyard high jump and middle school softball.

After our morning activities, the older kids would round up us young ones, and we would head to Mission Street to have our lunch. The Vega boy, Eric, had stumbled upon a place that doled out hot lunches for kids on summer weekdays, so we were regulars until it eventually became the site of a discount furniture store. I realize now that during those summers, we were participants in the Summer Food Service Program, a descendant program of Truman's 1946

National School Lunch Act. I didn't see it as a handout, though, maybe because I never felt poor; poor were the African kids on TV with distended bellies and flies around their mouths. For us, those meals were just a nice change, getting to choose between chocolate and white milk, and having something different for lunch every day like spaghetti or hot dogs or turkey cubes with mashed potatoes and gravy. It beat the peanut butter or tuna or bologna and white bread we were left at home, and the fruit trinity my mom believed in: apples, oranges, and bananas; the only fruit I remember eating as a child.

Our bodies fueled, we would begin our afternoon adventures in the Mission, or sometimes drop a nickel in a Muni bus coin slot and venture out to other parts of the city. On hot days we would go to Mission Pool, known by the locals as "Nickel Pool" (a misnomer by that point because inflation had made it cost a dime to get in), and swim to our hearts' content. One time, my active-duty sailor father sent us two emptied out nut cans filled with silver dollars that we were told to save because they'd be worth something some day. They were worth something, all right! We used them all to ice skate at a rink in the Avenues. I was Dorothy Hamill until the coins ran out.

One afternoon, Eric, who acted as our group scout ant, told us he found some cool vehicles for us to ride. We marched behind him one by one, hurrah, hurrah! Up the hill on Liberty Street, our same block, we walked into an ungated backyard, and found a goldmine of riding toys for all of our ages. The oldest ones found some banana-seated bikes, and we younger ones got the Flintstone-powered ride-on toys, clearly too small for us but we made it work. We took these new wheels and rode them with our legs straight out down our hill over and over again; this was long before the current speed bumps were installed. That night we parked our new vehicles in our apartment's garage area that had plenty of space since none of our moms had cars.

The next day, we were riding down the hill when we heard an angry white man yell, "Hey, you've got our toys!" As if we all had fugitive genes in our legs, we abandoned the toys on the street and ran like suspects in an episode of *COPS: Juvenile Edition*. The youngest of our group, Boris, lagged behind, crying that he wasn't going to make it, so Brianna swooped him up and ran with him in her arms like a soldier carrying a wounded comrade. We were like that: we always looked out for each other. We hid quietly in the closet of the B's apartment until Eric told us the coast was clear, probably about an hour. When we went back out onto our block, to the scene of our crime, the mean man was gone, but so was our new-to-us transportation.

While most of our afternoon fun was had outdoors, sometimes we would stick close to home. One day in particular, we younger ones decided to go back to the B's apartment and jump on their two queen beds, which were both in the one bedroom of their apartment. Our own room had a bunk bed and a single bed, so it wasn't something we could do easily at our place. We jumped for hours, flipping like gymnasts and touching our toes like collegiate cheerleaders. We even performed circus acts for each other. Introducing... for your viewing pleasure...the Amazing Alejandra! If we bonked our head on a wall, we wouldn't cry or have a store-bought boo-boo bunny ice pack to numb us. Instead, we would get right back up and rejoin the fun.

I guess our laughter was inviting because the older ones came downstairs to see what we were doing. The three older girls decided to watch while putting on some of Savannah's make-up and perfume. Eric, on the other hand, decided to join in. His jumping added a catapult effect to the activity. Betty, Boris, and I took a fearful break and became Eric and Alejandra's audience as he made her fall over and over again. Alejandra was enjoying all the wild falling until we heard a crash through the bedroom window. Alejandra's four-foot body was partially outside when Eric quickly pulled her in as if it were in the show's script. A loud silence filled the room like none we had ever experienced. We all knew she could have died. We all went back to our respective apartments, and I ate cornflakes and bananas the next morning.

With each passing summer, we all grew and so did our appetite for new activities. At one point, we discovered the unexplored world of arcade video games. *Space Invaders, Frogger,* and *Ms. Pac-Man* became different worlds we could enter through a portal at the corner store for the low price of a quarter. The problem: we didn't have too many quarters. The solution: one afternoon, Eric ran into our apartment and dashed to the back strip of cement that was our apartment building's version of a backyard (the other families only had fire escapes). He had a wooden hammer in one hand and a bag of nickels in the other. We all circled him as he gleamed about what he learned from some guy somewhere. He laid a nickel on the cement, and proceeded to hammer Jefferson's face into nothing. We marveled at the destructiveness of the activity and begged for our turn at whacking our third president's profile. After all the nickels were flattened, he then summoned us to follow him to the corner store arcade. We gathered around him as he shushed us so as not to call attention to ourselves. Eric then dropped in one of our new faceless coins and began invading space.

Later, back at our building, Eric cautioned us that we would get in big trouble if we were caught doing this and maybe even end up at YGC (Youth Guidance Center, San Francisco's euphemistic name for their juvenile hall). We all knew what YGC really meant: "You Got Caught." Eric's warning didn't scare us. One quarter turned into five thanks to Stanley, our trusty hammer. We never got caught for any of it. I sometimes wonder what the person emptying the coin boxes thought when he saw these mutilated coins. To him I would say, "I'm sorry for the slugs."

I haven't seen the B's in decades since their family moved out to Daly City. I also learned years later about the sneaky side of some men: Mr. Wonka ended up having a Mrs. Wonka at home. The rest of us kids went on to trade schools and/or colleges. We have had careers in the health field, childcare, social services, human resources, education, restaurant ownership, sports organizations, and the arts.

We are all homeowners, and most of us are parents now. One, my sister, just become a grandmother for the second time. We are all alive and, as far as I know, law-abiding citizens. Two of the mothers, including my own, still live in the same apartments, hoping they don't catch on (gentrification) fire.

Only within the past decade have my sisters and I shared with our aging mom all the details of what really happened during the summers when she was at work at the bank. We always seem to be around a large dining table at some family event, each one of us in our forties now, each contributing a detail to our collective memories. The only two words our mom can muster when we tell her the stories of our youth are, "No kidding!"

How to Become No One

Raluca Ioanid

First, leave your country. Abandon everything you know and love. Walk for seventeen days across the Sonoran Desert. Drink your own urine to stay alive. Arrive in Tucson through a hole in a barbed wire fence. Start from scratch. Completely blank. Become a man with no language. No family. No friends. No job.

Head north to San Francisco where you've heard you can start as something besides a farmworker. Hitch rides and take Greyhound buses buying tickets with the crumpled dollar bills that were pressed into your hand by everyone you know the days before leaving your hometown of Nayarit, Mexico.

The first nights in San Francisco you rent a room in the cheapest place you can find, the grimy Mission Hotel on South Van Ness and 16th. You wander the supermarket aisles of your new country agape at the dizzying excess and buy nothing. You try to order a cup of coffee at the gas station but the attendant who can't understand your accent, stares back at you with a blank dough-face. You eat donuts for dinner. You count out the last of your dollars and know that in three more days you will be on the streets.

You remember your grandmother and all the hope she had for you. The way she would cluck approvingly about your accomplishments to anyone who would listen, "*m'ijo tan inteligente.*"

Looking around at your dingy room with its peeling paint and cracked linoleum floor you wonder how the hell you are going to make it in this godforsaken place. "Tomorrow, I'll find work," you promise yourself. Back home you were the best in your class, the first to complete the equations in calculus class, the captain of the debate team, on track to go to medical school, the beloved eldest brother. But something always nagged at you, a knowledge that you were different, that the edges of this small town could not contain you. In Nayarit, a man cannot love another man.

Here, you are no one. You understand, but your English is heavily accented. You apply for a job at the same gas station where the woman wouldn't give you a cup of coffee. "No *papeles,* no job. We don't hire illegal aliens here."

Illegal. Alien. You think of astronauts in outer space, every ounce of oxygen measured, the scarcity of food, the enormous space between out there and home. You feel the boredom and the loneliness that comes after the initial euphoric rush of leaving. You see how you are like an astronaut whose oxygen is depleted, whose freeze-dried food store is at its end.

The social worker at the migrant worker center tells you that if you can prove you were the victim of violence or persecution in your country, you can apply for political asylum. You remember the taste of blood in your mouth, the bits of gravel and glass that lodged themselves into your cheekbone while you were being kicked in the ribs, all the times you were beat up because you loved someone you weren't supposed to love. You never imagined that so much pain would allow you to apply for a green card.

You get a job on the grill line at a taqueria on Folsom Street. They pay you five dollars an hour under the table, a stack of wrinkly, damp bills from the tip jar at the end of every shift. Your t-shirts all stink like fried meat and lard grease. You think you'll never eat another burrito again. You move into a dilapidated apartment on San Jose Avenue that you share with eleven people struggling to find their footing, just like you.

You sign up for English classes at City College where you practice sentences that are exercises in the absurd. You stumble over sentences about Bill and his yellow polka-dotted tie ordering hamburgers at a revolving restaurant. Your English teacher, Gabi, seems to believe that you are special and capable, she teaches you to watch American movies with the Spanish subtitles on. You do this to learn American English with its garbled potato-in-the-mouth diction. At work you practice keeping your mouth just so to get the accent right as you ask the customers, "What kind of beans would you like, pinto or black? Salsa, mild or spicy?"

You send Western Union money orders to Nayarit every week, sometimes $50, sometimes $100. Every Sunday you call home. "*M'ijo has encontrado use buena mujer?*" and politely endure questions about when you will be returning home with a good wife.

After work every night you go to the Castro. Here you see men who look like you, nut-brown skin, dark hair, almond shaped eyes, walking hand in hand, drinking and dancing at bars that spill into the street. You find comfort in these bars, in the strong cheap whisky drinks, and sometimes smart, always sexy men who want to get naked with you. At first you'd hoped for something more substantial but soon you become accustomed to a blur of different beds and different men. You find your way to the Latin clubs El Rio and Esta Noche, watching drag queens lip sync to the old Celia Cruz songs your *abuelita* loved.

For the first time in your life you are just like other people. You have crossed a continent and become no one for permission to be you. You decide you like San Francisco.

Mr. Belly's Interpreter

El intérprete del señor Barriga

Jorge Argueta

Teto's house on 24th Street in the Mission was where many of the Salvadorans came after they fled the civil war in El Salvador, 1980. It was good to have that house where we could rest and talk openly about our joys and our nostalgia.

Mr. Belly. That was what we affectionately called Chaín's father. The old man had come here fleeing the war in El Salvador in 1980. His children were all guerrillas, one of them had been captured and was in prison, and Mr. Belly had to leave the country for fear of being killed.

Don Belly would walk around picking up aluminum cans from the street to sell to the collection centers. He'd drink beer, and he'd spend the afternoons in the house telling stories about Cojutepeque, his hometown back in El Salvador.

One day he started groaning and complaining.

"What's wrong?" we asked him.

"Well," he said, a little embarrassed, but needing to vent about his pain, "my balls are swollen."

"Ah, well," we said, as if it was something quite normal, "let's go to the hospital."

At first he told us he didn't want to go because they take a lot of time there. He said they were going to take even longer because he didn't speak English.

"Don't worry!" I said. "Come on, that's no problem. I'll be your interpreter."

"Oh!!" he said. "That's true! I forgot this Jorgito speaks fine English. Yes, yes, with an interpreter, we can go."

We set off for the hospital that afternoon. The emergency room was three-quarters full; it was like all the drunks and drug addicts had agreed to get sick on the same day or had come there to get off the cold streets or both.

"Ay— ay ayyyyy, ayyyy ayyy," the hospital seemed to cry, its breath smelling of bleach and medicine.

Mr. Belly said to me, "Shit, this is just like Rosales," the hospital in El Salvador. He looked a little frightened. I did, too.

At last our turn came in the line where the patients receive a preliminary exam, have their temperature taken, and are asked why they had come to the emergency room.

The nurse was a young woman, her blonde hair like corn silk resting on her green smock, the stethoscope on her neck curved around like a little black snake with a round, shiny head. The nurse was very bright and very pretty. When our turn came, she asked, "Do you need a translator?"

"No," I replied confidently. Oh shit, I thought, the time has come to show off my English. Mr. Belly looked at me, his eyes a little sad but trusting. Everything was going great: name, address, age. This is easy, I thought. Mr. Belly felt reassured when he heard me speak in English, and at some point, when I asked him for his address, he was fully convinced of my qualities as an interpreter.

"She's asking what your address is," I told Don Belly. The gentleman looked at me with admiration, no doubt thinking, I have nothing to worry about, Jorgito's English is great.

Suddenly the young nurse asked the question of the afternoon: "And now, what is wrong with him?"

"Ahhhh," I said, immediately realizing that I had no words in the English I knew to describe Mr. Belly's ailment. I froze momentarily. I simply didn't know how to translate that the man had swollen testicles. Without thinking twice, I held up my hands on either side of my head, and spreading my fingers wide as I lifted them up and down in front of my face, I said loudly: "His balls are swelled up this big!"

The nurse looked at me, and it seems she understood quite well. She burst out laughing. Everyone around us laughed, and Mr. Belly and I laughed, too.

Amapola

Anna Maria Smith

My father enjoyed watching *Amapola,* the weekend Filipino variety show on Channel 18 hosted by Ness Aquino and Amapola, a local celebrity who wore a beautiful Filipino dress and sang for her TV audience in the '70s. The show was simple and featured some Taglish banter between the singer and her dashing host, both sitting in high-backed rattan chairs.

The Filipinos of my father's generation had come to the US decades before, first stepping onto heavy brown Hawaiian soil to work as laborers on the farms. As they made their way to the mainland, most settled near the coast. A good share of them chose San Francisco, where a little stretch of Filipino town existed. By the time I was ten, Manilatown had nearly disappeared and its last residents were in the middle of a fight against the forces of redevelopment to save the International Hotel, a residence for many of the older Filipinos and the last property of their own.

As Filipino Americans began to fight back against their eviction, Ness Aquino became an important figure for them. His Filipino supper club, the Mabuhay Gardens, was only a few blocks away on the long stretch of Broadway, an innocuous white building among a strip of flashing lights from the enticing stripper bars.

My father knew of Ness as his free time was spent at the International Hotel with his friends; they joined the I-Hotel protests. At home, my father invited me to watch *Amapola*. My mother had inexplicably banned Filipino things from our household, but *Amapola* was a way for me to learn some my father's culture and of his fight. *Amapola* was never a place for political issues, but her beautiful voice drifted into my father's psyche, and it let me know what he was missing. Nevertheless, I really wanted to watch something else on television.

I never connected my father's fight for his friends or his culture until years later, when I made my first trip to the Mabuhay Gardens to see the Dead Kennedys. I knew Ness on sight as the co-host of *Amapola,* and I shared this much with him as we chatted by the club's pinball machine. Ness wanted to know why I was at a punk show and I gave him the shortcut version of my ambition to be a rock journalist. The local punk music scene was original and shared my desperation for life. Ness wanted to help. He offered to open his club to me, promising that he would never charge me admission so that I could see my dream come true. He would greet me whenever I walked into my club, letting all my friends in without ever asking for money. Ness masked my awkwardness by bringing me backstage. He would introduce me to friends, and sometimes to the musicians. The rest was up to me but Ness knew who I needed to meet. He enabled those encounters, and I was soon making my way through a maze of loud music and show posters.

Over time, Ness would become like a second father to me. He was so happy when I became a DJ at college radio station KUSF, doing anything to accommodate us as we set out to conquer the world.

Our evenings were spent listening to new bands and fighting for some light so we could scribble notes onto napkins and little writing pads. We used the Mabuhay Gardens to make small films, take alleyway photos, and throw benefits. Ness continued to give and we thrived because of it.

There were times when I tried tell my father about Ness and the Mabuhay Gardens, but he never grasped the whole Filipino-restaurant-turned-punk-club transition – there was a fifty-year difference between us. I just wanted my father to understand that years of reluctantly watching *Amapola* had finally led to something positive. He remained under the impression I would be making a guest appearance on the show. At least he seemed proud.

The Stud

Patsy Creedy

Dancing used to be something I did, something we all did, something we carved out time for on a regular basis. It was a good night if my clothes were drenched in sweat. In a gay bar where there were no men to fend off, I was a gauzy dancing sylph free from my own ego to get lost and not a little drunk. I came to the Stud to dance, to drop my awkward burgeoning adulthood of waitressing and still attending San Francisco State on the eight-year plan (thanks for asking). I danced with my friends, our failures disappearing into the deafening music that momentarily displaced the anxious uncertainty of youth, our broken young hearts, and our post-adolescent funk at how hard it was to actually be an adult: paying rent month after month, rushing to get out of bed still half-drunk to the drone of the street cleaner and its meter maid accomplice.

We needed to move our bodies, to feel the music, to be with other people, those we considered our tribe, packing onto the dance floor, stripping off layers of clothing not in a totally sexual way but because we were hot from the exertion and the exhilaration we found in moving. No need to speak, other than mouthing the lyrics that connected us all in that moment. The dance floor was always packed but you learned to flow with the crowd, to allow a kind of physical touch and space that didn't or wouldn't normally be there. Dancing created a dreamy perimeter that swerved and undulated, full of sweaty forms crammed onto the tiny floor where we expressed our animal-ness, prone to howling, free in the forest for just a few hours.

I had a pair of bottle-green snakeskin pants and my friend David the dancer frequently borrowed them to go to the Stud. He couldn't zip them up all the way and that was just fine, in fact it was better. He wore his standard black tank top, which was usually lost or off by the end of the night. Hanes, I think. He bought them in bulk.

We sometimes walked to the Stud from my high school friend's house at Fell and Laguna. We would head out the door in our careful '80s dance attire, a tribal unit decked out in tight jeans and boots and flimsy tee shirts and filmy dresses. My hair was Sun-In blond and geometrically shorter on one side, where I sported a single large dangling earring. We were young and precious. We thought we had our finger on the pulse of the city, of our time.

The music we heard there was brand new, not yet on the radio, back when the radio was the primary vehicle for music. I remember hearing Tears for Fears and Soft Cell at the Stud way before they were on the radio. The guitar and drums at the beginning of "Everybody Wants to Rule the World" was the perfect mix of measured movement, the hint and slightly saddened promise of more: *welcome to your life, there's no turning back.* The resigned lament of the singer's voice capturing the yearning we all felt for some unknown time or place that was going to make everything come together. Song lyrics were able to encapsulate the misplaced surprise of the melancholy of finally being free and yet feeling so lost, too.

Disco was a mainstay at the Stud and oldies had their place, too. I usually had to have had a couple of drinks before I would be so bold, but I remember climbing up on the back of a chair to make a request at the DJ booth that was near one of the pool tables. The chair was one of those restaurant chairs, maybe from some forest green wallpapered steak house, covered in overstuffed shiny nauga-hyde with a brass-studded border on the back. I could not wait for any of my friends to spot me, I had to get to the DJ now. The people playing pool did not pause except to consider their next move and surprisingly no one ever fell. The DJ would always listen, leaning his head in to hear all the drunken, meaningful requests, and often he would play people's songs. Then we'd swarm anew onto the dance floor, giving him a two-armed wave as we danced, arms high in the air, sweat dripping down our backs.

No one was going to accidentally stumble into the Stud when it was on Folsom Street. SoMa was not a thing yet. Going to the Stud was like going somewhere in the Tenderloin, like the 181 Club, a black gay drag bar that had a white dance party night on Thursdays. It was a close second in my favorite dance places from those days. No bachelor parties or guys in from the Midwest looking for some local color were going to be anywhere near South of Market, which was then a place of wide empty streets filled with warehouses, car repair garages, and rundown flats. South of Market was iffy, full of drug dealers and doers, best to have somewhere to be, keep moving and don't get lost. The only restaurants in the area were Hamburger Mary's and a few late-night Chinese diners. The scattered leather bars and gay bars had found a neighborhood where people could be left alone in the dingy south of Market streets.

We sometimes went to the Mabuhay Gardens when punk was emerging. I remember my ex-husband slam-dancing as I watched horrified and hoping it didn't show. I never could connect with the cold nothing-matters kind of vibe and violence of punk. I still hate Joy Division to this day, picturing so many lost young boys falling further into the dark, when the light was just right there at the Stud. We saw countless terrible bands and drank illegal dollar beers in red plastic cups pumped from kegs. We saw self-conscious performance pieces and people between cars and behind dumpsters doing drugs and having sex. We just kept ending up at the Stud.

Then there were the bathrooms. There were two stalls right next to each other at the back of the club, across from the coat check. They had tiny saloon-style doors about three feet high, covering just enough, so you could always see who was in the bathroom, even squatting women. I remember seeing two guys in the stall next to me: I guess I didn't avert my gaze soon enough and my eyes met one of the guy's when he opened them for a second, winked at me, and went back to what he was doing.

After that I lived in fear of seeing guys fucking in the stalls, no way to move out of their sex space and pretend it wasn't happening. It was happening. But my discomfort at such close proximity morphed into mere irritation at having to wait to pee. I knew people were using the bathrooms for various activities and that was ok with me. I just wanted to use the restroom quickly so I could keep dancing and drinking. I felt I belonged at the Stud as much as any gay man. I could walk in the door and head to the back where the dance floor was, past men holding their black lit glowing gin and tonics, talking, kissing, pressing themselves against the wall, against each other, playing pool. It was all there and shifting to hold me as well as I took off my coat and listened to the music. I left enough of my sweat on that dance floor to be part of the family, absorbed into the faded wood floorboards.

The Stud was its own campy, sweet, and sometimes cranky universe: men in full drag pouring drinks, shirtless men with large nipple rings dancing to Donna Summer, and so many beautiful men hooking up and breaking up. There wasn't really any violence, in the masculine barroom brawl kind of way. There was the drama of betrayal and rejection, but it seemed there was an unspoken force field of understanding that the Stud was a haven, a place were you could be who you wanted to be, kissing that cute guy from across the bar who really was smiling at you.

There were leather boys, men in tight jeans, bears, chiseled Eastern Bloc muscle men, and a lot of women, gay or straight, more than in most gay bars in the City at the time. People came to dance, they came to watch, they came to play, they came to get laid, they came to feel real, birds finally nested with their kind.

I used to go back to my suburban hometown for Christmas dinner. I remember being at my high school friend's parents' house, and he and I looking at each other across the room signaling it was time to go, to go to the Stud and dance, to celebrate making it through another Christmas, back in our twenties when family was a mysterious, irritating, painful thing, a chore that we just had to endure. The gifts of belonging further down the road, if at all.

Many nights we danced until closing time and the lights came up. We were all still on the dance floor sweaty, still moving as the music changed to "Greensleeves," the sad dirge they often played at the end of Fillmore concerts. I remember one time as I headed over to the coat check at the end of the night, I saw a guy they called Paris putting his coat over the new leather jacket I had recently bought at Goodwill. I was still thrilled with the find.

"Hey, I think that's my coat," I said.

He looked at me and then down at the jacket with a surprised expression and said something like, "Oh, right," like he had no idea how my jacket could have found its way onto on his body. He handed me back the coat with a puzzled smile and we all left. I was perfectly happy to have my jacket back, no other action was required. We all laughed and made fun of what we were sure was a fake French accent and went across the street to Hamburger Mary's.

I don't remember making a decision to stop going to the Stud, maybe it was when I decided to move to the East Coast or maybe after I found out I was pregnant, or maybe it was my increasing difficulty with drinking that kept me away. I was shocked when I heard it had moved. It felt like the tarnishing of a childhood landmark that couldn't possibly be the same if it changed in any way, not realizing that the Stud, wherever it moved, was a refuge for other young people like me and my friends in the '80s, other people coming of age and feeling different and trying to find their people, trying to find out so many things about themselves and the world in a tiny haven filled with good music and glowing gin and tonics and a couple of pool tables.

I went to a drag show a couple of years back at the new Stud. It was a stretch for me to stay up late enough, but I promised a friend visiting from out of town that we would go. When I walked in a buzzing began in my head: This Stud was not my Stud. Where were the neon cocktails in their black light firefly splendor? Where was the wall lined with every array of gay incarnation, feather and leather and lots of skin, man, woman, or both? It felt like any other bar, a darkened room filled with drinkers who look up and then back to their drinks when they see that you who are walking in the door are not their savior, their fantasy in relief, walking in from the night and into their lives.

Then the drag show started and all the people in the bar — including me, now a divorced, middle-aged woman with two teenaged kids at home — became a unit; a laughing, cat-calling, clapping entity watching the glittery, oh so fabulous performers with their arching sky-high eyebrows and sculpted Rothko cheekbones, with their rhinestone encapsulated bodies like shiny larvae, night blooming right there, pantyhosed and stomping in their size 12 pumps, and at least one boa trailing and touching some lucky person in the front row. I was once again folded into the arms of the Stud, held and part of, dancing and sweating as if no time had passed, as if no one had died, no one had been hurt or othered by the inevitable hardness of the larger world. We were a we, in the hot close air of the Stud.

Station 40

Dee Allen.

It was the winter of 2012 when the Vara Apartments went up on 15th and Mission in the Mission District: the beginning of condo construction and skyrocketing rents citywide. High-speed redevelopment begins. Mayor Ed Lee invited the information technology industry to set up shop in SF. Twitter, Zynga, and other companies based their operations there. By the fall of 2013, Ellis Act evictions increased citywide, especially in the Mission District.

That November, my ex-housemate Irish told the residents of Anarchist social center/collective house Station 40 that our building's landlord was thinking about getting out of the landlord business. The S40 collective was given one year to leave prior to her selling off the building. I was the last to get the news, as always. The S40 collective — my housemates — wasted no time in organizing searches for new places, negotiated their time of stay while doing so, and searched for new lawyers to represent us in court since our initial representative eventually sided with the landlord and later proposed having our building sold to a community land trust.

At one Monday night house meeting, I'd used the suggestion of writer/musician friend Mitch Park: have Station 40 be registered with the city as a historical landmark. Our building, as the wooden sign that hung over the dining tables in the big space suggested, was the original Mission District post office. The post office that exists now has been on the corner of South Van Ness and 23rd Street since the 1960s. My housemates wanted to stay and fight their eviction; I wanted sorely to leave because I no longer had that fight in me. I wasn't going to fight for a hole-in-the-wall walk-up on 16th and Mission, where no one liked me or had my back. A shithole where I'd lived with fourteen or fifteen other adults and four or five pets. Small wonder it smelled of cat piss and dog shit half the time. I used to come there strictly for events long before becoming another tenant. After being a tenant, it's like my voice, my presence, and my vote at house meetings and public events never mattered to those so-called anti-authoritarians. I wanted out hella bad.

Exactly a year later, one afternoon in our kitchen, one of my housemates told me about being approached by Tiny from POOR Magazine during the Howard Zinn Book Fair at Mission High School down the street. No doubt, she had heard about our place being threatened with eviction. Tiny knew that I lived at S40. She gave a message to my Queer housemates specifically addressed to me: if I need a place to stay when S40 undergoes eviction, come to Homefulness in Oakland. I was glad the one housemate told me that; the other one didn't tell me shit. I made damn sure I committed that message to memory.

In the new year, 2015, the landlord decided to go through with the eviction. All of the S40 collective's suggestions were heard and refused. One telephone call to Tiny on the morning after the emergency house meeting helped give me a Point B to move to. It was just a matter of letting the Martin Luther King birthday weekend pass smoothly.

Five days later, with Oakland poet/teacher/builder/dancer Muteado Silencio's help, moving day commenced. I tore down the rope-tied bamboo wood rod/stapled black vinyl curtain, and emptied my loft, top and bottom. All of my belongings, boxed and loose, including some silverware, a black cast-iron skillet, and dishes stolen from the communal kitchen, were stored in the back of his white pick-up truck. The rest were pulled out of that padlocked bike hallway closet and added to the load. Upon completion, I laid my four house keys on the big space table top. Muteado and I drove away from that shithole, with my stuff in the back tied down with reddish rope. Five years of bullshit ended there. I moved out of Station 40, the Mission District and San Francisco. For good. No goodbyes for either place. I felt relief as we drove over the Bay Bridge. It's hard to feel sentimental when you're being forced out of your once-beloved adopted city of twelve years.

Point B: Homefulness. I moved everything of mine from Muteado's pick-up truck into the little house in back built by POOR Magazine folks old and young, with help from Decolonize Academy's four "youth skolaz." There I live, by myself. No more sharing refrigerator and cupboard space with housemates. No more labeling my food and beverages. No more leaving marker messages of any kind on a white dry-erase board. No more cleaning up after other people and their pets. No more practically standing in line to use the bathroom shower in the morning. No more playing host to others' guests. No more fighting fruit flies and bed bugs. No more noise complaints from whiny yuppie neighbors. Five years of collective living never agreed with me. Homefulness, Eastmont, Oakland. Love the land, love my house. Loathe the 'hood: what it is, where it is, and its sordid reputation. At least there are more Black faces here besides mine. I no longer feel like a victim of landlords but I don't feel like a revolutionary either. And Homefulness is a revolutionary project, formed as a solution to eviction, displacement, and homelessness. It's like I stepped out of one political battle and entered one more.

Conversation with a Buffalo

Tony Robles

When I was a kid, my father would make me sit with him and watch old western movies on TV. Those movies would be aired in the afternoon; cowboys on horses shooting at things: other cowboys, stagecoaches, whiskey bottles, and, of course, Indians. I looked more like an Indian than a cowboy. My dad would sit, his attention, his mind, his spirit inhabiting each scene as if he'd been on horseback with a six-shooter firing into the expanse of sky as the wild prickly cacti bore witness. I'd see horses, badges, tumbleweed, and gamblers on our little TV set but there was one thing I never saw: buffalo. "*Oh, give me a home, where the buffalo roam...*" the song went. Where were the buffalo?

All the classic westerns those afternoons with the old man and not a single buffalo, not even a mound of buffalo shit, on the small screen. There has to be a buffalo, one hanging around somewhere. So one day I left and went looking for one. I get lost all the time. I have no sense of direction, especially if someone gives me directions. If

I'm told to turn left, I will turn right. I found myself in Golden Gate Park—how I got there, I don't know—I just put one foot in front of the other, my mind guiding me in a daydream without direction. It was at Golden Gate Park that I came upon buffalo! Four or five of them, fenced in. I stood outside the fence gazing at them. They stood chewing as the sky above seemed to move.

I called out, "Hey, buffalo!" but they ignored me.

"Hey, buffalo!" I said again.

"Get lost, kid," a voice called out.

I looked at their skin, a burnt brown with patches of wooly growth. I stayed for an hour before going back home where my father was still watching that old western.

I am all grown up now, a reporter for Poor News Network (PNN). I still live in San Francisco but many people I grew up with are no longer here. I recently visited Golden Gate Park to seek an interview with one or more of the buffalo in their refuge called the Golden Gate Park Buffalo Paddock. It was my sincere hope to learn of their feelings about the city, about life, and, it was my hope that I wouldn't be told to get lost.

"Hey, buffalo!"

"I thought I told you to get lost."

"That was you?"

"I might be a buffalo, but I got the memory of an elephant. I never forget a face. So, are you still watching those lousy western movies?"

"No, that was a long time ago," I reminded him.

"All lies anyway. So many buffalo killed."

"What have you been up to?" I asked him.

The buffalo looked up at me. Its face was huge, so huge that if I threw a punch at it with my eyes closed from any angle—overhand right, left hook or a punch launched from between my legs—I'd surely hit something.

"I've been here, on the land," the buffalo replied. "The land has always been here. People change, come and go, but the land is here. But I'm worried, the way it's going, I hope I don't get evicted. I even had one goofy son of a bitch that came around the other day. He asked if I was renting this place as an STR. STR... what the fuck is that? Some kind of sexual transmitted disease among buffalo? 'Short term rental,' the guy says. Damn colonizers, didn't they spread enough of that around? Shit, these folks just got here yesterday and they're asking me if I'm living in a short term rental. Then he told me that I could make some bread by listing this place on some shit called Airbnb. I told him, 'I don't need no Airbnb because the air I breathe is good and I can shit wherever I damn well please. But the guy kept hanging around being a pain in the ass. Home on the motherfuckin' range ain't what it used to be, I guess."

The buffalo's mouth moved in a chewing motion, masticating air mostly, out of habit. It looked into the sky. A smear of fog blocked the sun. The buffalo yawned and proceeded to lay a long, glorious, graceful shit on the thick patch of grass at its feet.

"What's changed in the city?" I asked.

"Well, who are all those goofy motherfuckers with beards running all over the place? They all look like General Custard."

"You mean Custer?"

"Custer, Custard... What difference does it make? Someone should airlift some razorblades and drop 'em. All them beards running around like something out of Burning Man. To me, it's a bunch of burning bullshit."

"They come around a lot?" I wondered aloud.

"Yeah, standing by the fence, trying to get my attention, snapping pictures on their little phones. They're like flies landing on the ass of a warthog, swarms of them. You just want to swat them. I tell you, brother, if this fence wasn't here..."

At that point, I felt a vibration emanating from my pants pocket. It was my cell phone. I pulled it from my pocket. Before I could answer the call, it was swatted from my hand by a quick swipe of the buffalo's tail landing on the mound of shit a foot or so away. It seemed like my cue to ask, "You ever try to escape?"

"I did, years ago. But I ain't no kid no more. If I tried that now they'd call the cops and that would be my ass."

"The cops are out of control," I agreed.

"Damn right they are. What they did to that kid Mario Woods was a damn shame. It was an execution. They need to fire the police chief. What's his name, Slur?"

"I think it's Suhr..."

"Well, I sure as hell ain't calling him 'sir.' Aesthetically, he ain't lookin' too good. Resembles head cheese under a heat lamp. But, yeah, the cops are off the hook. And what's the mayor doing? He's pullin' a Wizard of Oz. We'd do better with all-you-can-eat Shrimp Boy, at least he'd set us up with a little cheese bread, which is a helluva lot more than we get out of this mayor. And I heard about something called 'text messages' the cops were sending on their cell phones – a lot of racist stuff, oh yeah, slurs. But I ain't into cell phones... they're out of my range."

"How did you hear about it then?" I was getting really curious.

"I get the paper. Some of these old guys drop it off during their morning walks. Five cops shot that brother. That was wrong, just like they did Alex Nieto. But you know, they been shooting at us forever. So many buffalo slaughtered. So many brothers shot. Soon there will be no more brothers or sisters left in the city."

"The black population is 3% in the city now," I tell him.

"Damn shame. I've seen it. A lot of brothers used to come out here and we'd talk. Them guys were cool. One of 'em used to say, "Everything is everything."

"I've heard that one, too."

"It's true, everything is everything. We are connected to each other, to air and sky and water. Problem is that you got folks that think everything is theirs."

"Everything's everything?"

"Everything is everything"

"Any last words?"

"Yeah... Custer can kiss my ass."

A Tale of Three Cities

Broke-Ass Stuart

"After the past few nights, I've realized San Francisco is a tale of three cities," I say to the little group of people with whom I'm smoking and drinking. We're sitting on cushions in somebody's "zen room" at least a dozen floors above Market Street in the NEMA Building – a brand new high-rise apartment complex in the heart of the city. Given its proximity to so many tech companies, it more or less functions as very high-end dorms for tech workers.

"You see, the three cities are high rise, low rise, and no rise," I say. "'High rise' is obviously where we are now. It's the folks whose entire relationship to San Francisco is seen through the lens of making money from the tech boom. Those who live in the 'low rise' city are the people who were already here and are fighting to keep San Francisco a place for everyone. They generally don't live in high-rise buildings. And those that live in the 'no rise' city sleep in tents at the foot of the high-rises… It was the best of times, it was the worst of times, and it was the far, far worse of times."

I was a little stoned and a little drunk, but as far as semi-poetic generalizations go, it was pretty good, especially considering the previous few nights I'd had. A couple nights before I'd joined with thousands of other activists in shutting down 880. We were protesting the recent police murders of Alton Sterling and Philando Castile, and the hundreds of years of systemic violence that police have inflicted on communities of color. It was powerful and it was peaceful, and while I'm sure there were some high rise people there, it was mostly made up of low risers.

The night at the NEMA building was completely different though. It had started at the Modernist, a brand new private club where an annual membership costs $3000 and all you get is access to a bar and restaurant where a vodka soda will set you back $16. Nick and I were allowed in because we were there for somebody's birthday. The bar was full of tech industry millionaires for whom San Francisco was a gold mine. We left shortly afterward, chased out by incredibly expensive booze prices and offensive techno music, and headed to an apartment party at NEMA.

And it was there that it dawned on me that we really were living in three separate cities. This party was full of young, well paid tech workers who were most likely employed by people who are members of the Modernist. The only books on the shelves were about coding, and the biggest framed thing on the wall was a collection of stock certificates from some technology company. "Where the fuck am I?" I asked Nick. He works at a well-known tech company but has been in SF long enough to be part of the struggle to keep San Francisco, well, San Francisco. He's like a bridge between lower risers and high risers.

"Yeah, man, it's like I told you," Nick said. "A lot of these people may live and work in San Francisco, but they aren't actually in our San Francisco. They go to work, then go to restaurants and bars that primarily cater to tech money, then live in a building that only houses tech workers. It's like a parallel universe."

"Or a completely different city," I replied.

And worst yet, they were out of booze. So we went down to his friend's place to get some, and ended up in the "zen room" where I expounded my unified theory on our tale of three cities.

Skid Row is Still Skid Row (and Closer Than You Think)

Norman Antonio Zelaya

It was much colder in the apartment than it was outside, air coming from under the door filling the space to the high ceiling. I splashed cold water on my face, the chill lighting up my skin. I breathed in the biting air deeply. My bare feet were freezing on the stone tile. I looked at my ruddy face in the mirror. Fuck. It was 4:58 in the morning.

I threw on my sweatshirt, grabbed my keys, and headed for the door. "I want to go to the gym with you," said Melly.

The gate banged loudly behind us as we bounded onto the sidewalk. Melly took me by the crook of the arm and pulled me along. The wet street reflected the red, yellow and orange light of the street lamps and storefronts. It was dark. It was quiet. One car cruised by, wheels gently rolling over the pavement. Melly hugged me and brrrred into my neck. It was damn cold. She pecked me repeatedly then tweaked my nose.

We walked arm in arm in the pale fluorescent light of Mission

Street, close, tightening our embrace against the chilled air. Melly was spending more and more time at my place and we were doing more things together, daily things, like shopping for dinner and cooking and dropping off dry cleaning and now exercising. Melly was loving that. She was a swimmer in high school and missed being so active. She was having a good time doing things together.

"What are we doing today?" she asked.

"What do you feel like doing?"

"I want to work on *nalgas*." She grabbed a round cheek. "For real. I want to get in shape. I want to improve my curves. I want to work on being *hermosa*," she said.

"You are *hermosa*, Melly."

"I want to be *más hermosa*." She hissed her S's as she put her hands on her hips and turned her back to me. She stopped. "Oh my god..."

Laying against the wall next to the door of a small jewelry store, a man was perfectly still across the sidewalk. A white sheet was pulled up to his waist, his hands folded over it. His head was thrown back, his mouth slightly open like readying for a kiss. His eyes were closed tight, expectant, afraid, waiting for something terrible. Blood was spattered on the wall above his head like a feathery crown. Some blood had trickled from his nose; his lips were a bit darkened.

Many homeless people spent the night under the marquee of the old Grand movie theater or in that shallow doorway next to the jewelry store. It gave hardly any shelter but folks sought it out anyway. It was coveted as the sun set and the sky grew overcast, and that evening wind whipped through the corridor. They lay on cardboard, rolled up in blankets, or set up shopping carts around salvaged bedding and hunkered down for the night, sleeping while the hipster fucks and tech drones walked over them and by them on their way through the string of bars in the neighborhood. They slept through the shrieking of tires, and the whir and hiss of the buses. They slept through the chatter and mindless talk, and shouts and calls from across the street, and folks talking on their phones and laughing until it was late and folks were done drinking, the store lights blinking, and the last bus roaring down Mission. Then it was quiet, but cold. They slept through the cold, tugging at their blankets, turning on their sides.

This man was just another homeless person in a terrible way. He was not well and in need of help.

"What do we do?" Melly wanted to know.

"Fuck, I don't know."

"Is he just asleep? He's hurt."

"He's probably drunk. He's covered like he's sleeping."

"Someone will find him, right?" Melly asked hopefully.

I looked around. Mission Street was empty. No cars. One man at the corner waiting for the light to change, thumbs hooked on the straps of his backpack. No perceivable help anywhere. I pulled my phone out of my bag and dialed 911.

"Hello, I want to report a man in need of help. He's laying on the sidewalk and he's bloodied… I can't tell, he's really still… his face is all bloody… It doesn't appear that he's breathing but I haven't really checked… his mouth is bloodied…" I approached the man and tapped his covered heel with my toe. "He's not responding, he needs assistance... No, I don't know him... Okay... Please, thank you."

I turned to Melly. "They're sending a patrol car to check him out."

"So do we wait?"

I thought about it. I was in schedule mode, my day planned out to the minute: get up early, go to the gym, type up a sub plan, email it, check in with my principal, then be at the Hall of Justice for jury duty by nine o'clock. This man needed our help, but I didn't know what else I could do, and I needed to stick to my plan. I didn't think any of the folks I had to answer to – the judge, my principal – would forgive my absence or tardiness because I stopped to tend to an injured, homeless man. I was bound to my duties. Fuck.

"They said police are coming. They'll know what to do. They can figure it out."

"But someone will come?"

"Yes, someone's coming. And if not, I imagine when the folks from the jewelry store open, they'll call the police, too."

"Poor man."

We backed away and continued walking down the street, holding hands.

On the other side of the street, a woman walked determinedly through the shadows and hurried across the wide expanse of South Van Ness. Back on the sidewalk, she continued her nervous quick pace toward Mission and the relative safety of the streetlights.

The sky was clear. Several stars shone bright, and many smaller stars could be made out. There were quite a few, considering we were in the middle of the city. I stopped to survey the sky. Melly leaned into me, an arm around my waist, as she pointed out the constellations.

"That is Orion's Belt. Those three little stars right there," she said. "And over here is Spica. Find the handle on the Big Dipper, arc to Arcturus, then spike down to Spica.

"How do you know how to find the stars?" I asked.

"Camp. That's what we do in the suburbs. We go to camp and look at the sky," she said.

"Where is the North Star?"

"It's way over there," she motioned, swinging her arm from one side of the sky to the other while stealing a kiss. "You can't see it from here. This building is in the way."

We walked through the dark shadows under the cherry and magnolia trees. It was getting colder so we picked up our pace. My car was still several blocks away.

After the gym, we drove quietly through the lightening streets. The sun was rising, the pink light falling on the hills below Twin Peaks. We passed a bottle of water between us. "Drop me off here. I want to go to the market and grab some things for dinner," she said.

I drove off to look for parking. I showered quickly, changed, and got to typing up my lesson plan for the sub.

"I wanted Italian sausage but el mercado doesn't know about the pleasures of Italy, so it's *chorizo de bola Salvadoreño* instead with penne pasta in a white sauce with snow peas and asparagus tips," Melly said as she set her bag of groceries on the dining table next to my laptop. I kept typing.

"That poor man died."

"Really?"

"Yeah. I saw the police putting him in a yellow body bag."

"Damn. That's a shame."

"It is. It's sad. A poor man is dead. And it's sad that he died all alone."

"That's terrible. I feel bad for him."

"Why did someone hurt him? He didn't have anything anyone wanted."

"Don't know. People are messed up. They do fucked-up shit to each other all the time."

"Fucking people."

"I have to go."

"What time are you getting out?"

"I don't know. It's jury duty. I imagine I could be there all day."

I double-checked my pockets for my keys, my ID, and change for the train. The street was cast in shadow, but the sun was up and the sky was clear blue. It looked to be the beginnings of a beautiful day. I walked by the jewelry store. The man was gone, his body taken away to be placed in some refrigerated locker. Tagged. Counted. Noted. The wall and sidewalk were scrubbed and washed. Nothing left but a white chalky substance smeared in circles where his body had lain. Nothing to know that he had spent the night there. The owner of the mercado lifted boxes of produce from the bed of his pick-up and stacked them on a hand-truck. The hip owner of the window café ground coffee as customers waited. Outside the fish market, workers hosed out large plastic bins and washed the runoff into the curb as the 14 Mission bus splashed to the stop to pick up passengers. There was nothing to know that a man had died in that shallow doorway early this morning. It was like he was never there.

When I got to the platform, my train was waiting to take me downtown. As a boy, I loved the train. I didn't take it very often. I hardly ever left San Francisco. I remembered the first time I rode it, I asked my mother how the train got to Oakland. She said it went into a tube that passed through the bay.

"It goes under water!?"

"*Sí, hijo.*"

I imagined the train going through a clear plexiglass tube, and large fish and rays and sharks swimming freely, roaming, turning suddenly then gliding gracefully, my brothers and I following them closely, watching them swim, our heads moving with each change in movement, our hands pressed firmly against the glass, as clear as if we were at the aquarium. I was disappointed when the train went into the tube and the windows went black and nothing happened except for the train howling and rocking until we came up over the desolate tracks of the reticulated train yards of West Oakland. Dry, dusty, filled with still, single cars.

I came out of the station at Powell and walked along Market, past the closed shops and empty storefronts, past what used to be the St. Francis movie theater and an arcade and Kaplan's Sporting

Goods store, where I bought a NY Giants baseball cap and batting gloves and a dozen wrist bands, enough to wear from wrist to elbow. All of this is shuttered and fenced by large sheets of plywood, pasted with large posters of the future mall set to be built in its place, a series of airy glass and steel polyhedrons for shoes and dresses and skin care – the future of shopping on Market Street.

On the following block, I walked past converted office spaces, twenty-foot tall panes of glass letting into narrow lobbies, live-work lofts, spaces shared by multiple hopeful start-ups, and one lobby, on second look, let into a trendy barbershop that offered shaves with a straight razor. To the right of the receptionist table was a spacious sitting room, the back wall was entirely shelved like a private library with a rolling ladder, and a large pool table sat in the middle of the floor. There were no chairs. Several people crossed my path, clutching the straps of small packs, and adjusting their earbuds. They pushed open the tall brass-hinged doors and ducked into the narrow hallways, no one ever making eye contact.

Steam rose through a manhole cover, the sunlight reflecting brightly on the plumes, shining on the wet asphalt of Sixth Street. I checked the time. I had twenty minutes to make it to the courthouse. Three men were set up in a doorway, resting on crates and sifting through duffel bags. They played music loudly from a boombox buried beneath all their things as they passed around a joint. A frail-looking woman came from across the street to shout at them about not finding Karla, that she just wasn't around, and didn't nobody know where she was at. Dude on the lowest crate rebuked her mildly, "I want my money, Wanda. That's all."

Wanda turned to the street, looking up and down the block, exasperated, stepping off the curb then back on, almost talking to dude on the crate but said nothing, then turned back to the hopelessness of the idle street, looking into the few cars that dragged past. A light drizzle began to fall so I picked up my pace.

Sixth Street was still lined with liquor stores and pawnshops and adult video stores. Dudes stood outside the doorways of the liquor stores and chatted, people walked in looking for change or other people – Where Louie at? He's not in yet. C'mon, man, where Louie at? Come back at noon – and they came out with brown bags, 40 ounces of beer, chips, cigarettes, lottery tickets. On the sidewalk, they meandered, took a small step to the side, inspected a crack, then returned to their original spot. They checked the pockets of their oversized coats, digging deep into the bottom trying to remember, spoke softly to themselves, checked the inside pocket, felt around the outside of their drab coats, trying to remember, even looked inside their beanies but could not remember where... what was it... checked furiously again but became more and more lost, frustrated, unable to bring back the thought, grumbling – I know I had it, I know I did, here, right here.

Others spoke loudly, forcefully, but not quite a shout. One dude came careening through the sidewalk, almost reckless, but navigating the other souls and their gear, the meters and garbage cans and hydrants, scaffolds and parking signs. This dude came too close as I walked by. He carried a bundle of clothes, and screamed as he zigzagged along. He looked at me and took an aggressive step in my direction. I watched him, but kept on walking. He stopped short, laughed, then trudged across the street giving a fuck about the traffic. Another dude smiled at me and said good morning. "Good morning," I answered back. He smiled and nodded like a sick parrot: good morning, good morning, good morning... The pawnshops were open but empty, except for the shopkeepers. The adult video stores were still closed.

"Do you have any spare change, sir?"

"No, I don't. Sorry."

I hurried to make the light. Then I stopped and checked my bag. I scraped around the bottom, underneath my magazine and sweater. I heard some clinking. I searched further and came up with two quarters.

"Here you go."

"Thank you, baby. Thank you. You have a good day."

"I will try."

I hurried on. Someone else reached out a bare hand, but I had nothing to give except "sorry" and a bashful smile.

I hustled across the five lanes of Harrison Street at the red light. Traffic was light and the blocks were hella long so I needed to make all the time I could. About half a dozen small tents were set up in the protection of the underpass, shopping carts carefully placed against them, keeping the openings free and accessible. Plastic tarps were extended between two larger tents covering some lawn chairs. These makeshift camps were more and more common in San Francisco. Potrero Hill. Folsom Street. Hayes Valley. Not just under freeways or in Golden Gate Park or other out-of-the-way, unwanted places. There were no more unwanted places. They have been coming for it all. Speculators. Developers. Venture capitalists. Techies. Gawkers. Conventioneers. Virtual realists. Temporary citizens. Believers in progress. They want all of it. Every bit. Every inch.

Two police officers stood outside, hands on hip and holster, directing, supervising, pointing with outstretched hands. They were making the settlers take down their tarps and disassemble their tents. A woman emptied bedrolls, bags of clothes, and comforters from a tent while her companion arranged them into the shopping carts. Others were busy untying twine and folding tent poles into small nylon bags, while a thin man wearing a gray Niners sweatshirt tried to reason with the police, calmly making his points with an open, polite hand. The police watched the others continue dismantling the camp as they listened. He spoke calmly, referring to their belongings, and then to the city with open arms: Where were they supposed to go? Where could they go? They were homeless; they weren't doing anything wrong. But they couldn't stay there. The camp was illegal. They were trespassing on city grounds. They were loiterers. Unlawful campers. They were transients, indigents, undesirables, riffraff. They were dirty, unclean. They left behind garbage. They were loafers, vagrants, drifters, repellent, unsavory, lowlifes, homeless, unwanted, illegal.

The thin man pled his case, pled for his companions, but the police had run out of patience. They shepherded him back with the others, and directed him to help get their things out quickly. Now. One police grabbed a couple of sleeping bags and dragged them to the curb. He banged on a shopping cart and demanded it be moved. Now. They were done talking. They were done listening. They were done.

Over the summer, two of my students joined the ranks of the homeless. Welfare takers. Anchor babies. Societal burdens.

Hmm. *Pobrecitos.*

Owl House, San Francisco's Finest

Michael Koch

Crack or crank, lubricated by bad vodka. Troves of unresolved trauma. Copious doses of self-doubt. Social disdain meet anomie. It's a bad recipe, a worse stew. Our mental health clients at the half-way house are not dressed for success in this world or the next. Their only hope is that all possible universes exist simultaneously, spinning dizzily in all directions. Yes, it's that bad — although, to be fair, Owl House does bear a curious resemblance to Club Med in that we, too, clients and staff, are often supine and stupefied on the edge of the deep blue sea.

The world is a kaleidoscope of disorienting peril, after all. I can dig it. I'm a fool for color. I'm a fool for tomfoolery. Clients come and go, every word a lie, every laugh and grimace teeming with truth. Each with an agenda that can't be paraphrased. Many responding to voices, alternately tyrannical, moronic, mythical, sublime. I come to work as if to a buried realm of non-being.

Owl House – a stylish three-story Victorian by Golden Gate Park in its long-ago heyday, now downgraded to what the City calls an Acute Diversion Unit, or ADU – once had 10 clients, about 15 counselors and administrators, a few nurses, a psychiatrist, intermittent student nurses, and maintenance people, plus an occasional visitor from the Central Office to menace and cajole the staff, explaining away the latest indignity, the latest policy run amok.

Now we have fewer staff, more clients (few now adequately screened or assessed), and endless paperwork related to nothing. The City and County of San Francisco is always threatening to cut the budget: mental health is a luxury we can't really afford, despite the fact that San Francisco might be the wealthiest city in the world.

Awkward tics, mine or theirs? The eternal recurrence of what never happened reoccurs pitilessly. Take J.: Resolutely nondescript, normal to a pathological fault, reeking with sincerity and insincerity, the tenuous pillars of wisdom. He's eager to show you his jagged abdominal scar, the delicate fissures where his mind leaks out. Maybe a 7-Eleven stick-up gone south. A moment of selfless heroism in Kuwait. A hapless self-evisceration after a disastrous prom night. His stories tend toward the improbably heroic, are inconsistent with one another, chronologically impossible, logically flawed, immaterial to the rough-hewn hell where the amateurs of oblivion gather.

J. has a megaton pain-management regimen, pure horsepower, *puro bandido*. He has to dose on methadone daily, early. He has been everywhere: all the hospitals, clinics, shelters, support-service hotels, acute-diversion units, halfway houses, each of which creates an elaborate computerized chart of lies, half-truths, misinterpretations, and, rarely, canny clinical insights. Everyone starts on the Tower of Babel from scratch.

J. has an alphabet of charts in his file. Chart A: Client saw his mother murdered by his stepfather. The primal wound that set this merde in motion. Chart B: Client lists his mother as his "emergency contact" person. *Madre mía.* Chart C: Client was recently traumatized by a blade-wielding maniac and shows hand wounds consistent with warding off a knife. Chart D: Client specified that his attacker was a half-witted giant in the employ of the CIA who pummeled him in the face with his fists.

On my afternoon break, already half-broken, I'm trying to sleep without drawing undue attention to myself. Are my dreams too obtrusive? Are they rude or noisy? It will take only a light knock to awaken me: You can breathe my name through the keyhole, summon me into alertness with a sigh. Actually, I'll still be dreaming, a ghostly evanescence bustling about as if I gave a rat's ass about the proverbial "other" at the threshold to what? Can I get a witness? Can I get some sleep? Does the "raveled sleeve of care" merit a stitch in time or am I on my own here? At least I'm feigning sobriety. A half pint of sobriety and I'll be good.

I told my mother, "Look, don't worry. The afterlife is nothing. It's just like now but with better wine, better weather, better everything. I mean, you think things could be worse than this? Fools everywhere? Suffering? Impermanence? Death?"

My schedule is a mosaic. The broken tiles add up to 40 hours a week, just enough to assure that my élan vital is on life support. I use a crutch, several aspirins, and a crypt beneath the floor suitable for heavy daydreaming. I trim my eyebrows with a blowtorch.

I do need a less stressful job, perhaps as a talking head or a mannequin. Something in petty crime or aesthetics might be nice. Sports betting is appealing because, as soon as the game is over, it's all so self-evident: Of course home-field advantage would be neutralized by the weather; of course, the role of overwhelming favorite would lull team A into a torpid complacency nothing could remedy. Of course, the umpire would refuse to call the low strike, the referee would permit blatant holding, humble crustaceans would fly out of the sea directly to a cerulean mountain top. If only I knew four hours or four months ago what I know now... if only my own madness were more strategic.

The "us" and "them" distinction is, after all, a dodge. We have some empty jargon for every aberrant gesture; everything is medicalized, pathologized, taken out of the context, which would incriminate and absolve everyone. First, what am I doing here? Is there a lucrative "elsewhere" behind Door #2? Should I credit providence, blame fate? Count my blessings before the really scary algorithms kick in? There's no surer, more glamorous path through the woods than the one not taken.

Nobody can really do this job, even a veteran counselor who combines the mojo of Freud, the zaniness of St. Francis, and the reassuring demeanor of a favorite grandparent. First, there's the ever-metastasizing paperwork needed to cajole bureaucrats from state licensing and Medi-Cal, the City auditors, and agents from the Inquisition. Here are the official platitudes, make liberal use of them, keep the day of reckoning at bay. Mention healthy self-care routines, hydration, nutrition, exercise, adequate rest, and appropriately expressed emotions. Throw in avoiding neighborhoods full of dope and predators, leopards and evangelists.

We'll help clients cauterize wounds before they fester. We'll provide historical perspective and hand-holding, penmanship lessons and clean socks. Some of us will be grammatical, others colloquial; some will bring arduously acquired wisdom to the party, others will play the neurotic self-indulgence card until the police come with Rorschach tests and stun guns. We'll encourage medication compliance and talk about suitable post-Owl-House 90-day treatment options.

Staff will provide structure and support, and facilitate groups about relapse prevention, managing auditory hallucinations, alleviating depression, and misspelling despair. Staff will help clients handle and ameliorate anger. We'll take them to peep shows to explore the allure of furtive self-revelation. We'll take them to a wine-tasting where the relative merits of several merlots will be discussed until everyone comes to blows.

The platitudes are necessary. Life is nothing without a song. I walk in the door fighting. Every fiber of my being bathed in torpor, reluctance, a suspicion that I should be elsewhere, in the vortex of my dreams.

But as I always say: At least I'm not embarrassed to tell anyone what I do. It sounds noble and enlightened, to be a first responder to the psychic fires under the surface of "normal" life. Underpaid, exhausted, rappelling down the crumbling edifice of the id to hunt for survivors. My hair is aflame. My ears are burning. My pants are running down the block ahead of me.

At least I'm not lionized and richly rewarded for grinding orphans into dust that I resell as "derivatives" or retailing the sweat of widows as an exclusive eau-de-cologne. I've been palling around with nothingness since knee pants.

So, one night, listlessly adrift in the shadows (all of us), a client famous for bludgeoning baby seals in the Arctic of his mind threatens to talk my head off, to make my coconut explode like a trick cigar. He's off-the-cuff, over-the-moon, babbling on, hedging his bets, teleporting his soul. Send in the clowns in full riot gear, I think my chromosomes are breaking into hives.

On and on he goes, *blah blah blah,* bad dope, suicide, a coerced confession, a foolish bet, *blah blah* innocence, *blah blah* guilt. "It's a conspiracy," he says. Manufactured evidence, recovered memories, an eyewitness account, *blah blah blah.*

At least the unintelligible narrative of Mr. Logorrhea is more compelling than the mountain of trivial paperwork I'm trying to finish as my mind starts its regimen of nocturnal backflips. He goes on:

police *blah blah,* eyewitnesses *blah blah,* a vendetta, some poisoned mouthwash, stolen cognac, a cheap trick, the police again *blah blah,* a circus of betrayal, a lottery of lies.

He said he was getting ultimatums from his tooth, which is in cahoots with the Chinese government. Who could sleep when every time he started to doze off a stranger in a tuxedo started whistling in his ear? And if he fell asleep, his cousin would steal his internal organs and try to pawn them. Or am I confusing his story with someone else's? I can't tell a *mensonge* from a mongoose.

One client watched her wheelchair-bound brother saw off his foot with a chainsaw. Later, asked about her mood, she said, "I see wooden horses, but there's no sky." Another client told me, "Your problem is you can't see what's not there."

Thank the lucky shamrocks for the delete button, the rewind, the strategic retreat. Feinting one way, staggering another. The choreography of a crab, going nowhere with leisurely panache, yet not quite.

Tired. Again and again.

Tired and retired incessantly, between flame-outs, incendiary routines that repeat themselves as farce, as tragicomedy on steroids smoking stale cigarettes. But don't forget to factor in the fleeting euphoria (as euphoria must fleeting be). They'll say we're lucky to have jobs, and joblessness will chase us down the street with empty eyes. Don't get angry. Get odd. Close your eyes fitfully. The lion will treat the lamb to a nice lunch, and then we'll all rush for the exits.

Yes, I'm counting the days but aren't my days already numbered? El Destino. How it hovers like an illuminating fog! Upon close inspection, any life appears to be an extenuating circumstance, a cruel joke whose caprice is written in stone. The damaged child becomes the damaging adult, the sins of the father just fit into the grandson's fever, packed nails in a bomb.

To pity others, we must be able to pity ourselves. The assembly-line belt only slows when it breaks. A certain Vladimir, no prophet, said ninety years ago, "Ethics will be the aesthetics of the 20th century." Last night, a client said, "My foot itches and I may have to hurt someone," and it was pure nihilist poetry. Our new century may eclipse even the last in its relentless momentum of self-immolation.

Something happens. And then, "to make matters worse," something else. We're always toying with the abyss, moving emptiness from one hive to another and getting stung. Every part of the whole is in free-fall as we dream parachutes of fluorescent silk.

As of yesterday, three clients were wearing Depends, a commercial euphemism for diapers that evokes the uncertainty that gives life its flavor, its odor of predestined randomness. Of course, there will be accidents and miscalculations and proverbial "acts of God." Soiled diapers will be found in mysterious places. Mystified finders of said diapers will come up with colorful theories: We will debate the possible roles of dementia, side effects from medications, untreated infections, bad luck, drug use, barometric pressure, astral configurations. We will brandish the term "sociopath" like a scourge as necessary (or when fatigue has vanquished our last illusion of compassion).

Fate and conflict are indispensable for a good drama. We have comfortable seats or, rather, strategically broken ones that sharpen our humanity and crack open our hearts until we leave the theater howling like little Artauds, little deposed princes.

Every day, things get worse and I enjoy myself more. The theater is jammed. The stage is littered with corpses. There are unintelligible monologues, a lot of spectators sneezing heedlessly. The trajectory of the play is pre-ordained yet open-ended. Failure, too, has a beauty that demands to flourish.

A Portrait in the Tenderloin

John Goins

It disturbed me to dream about my father, who was sitting with his old cronies on the porch of the house I grew up in. I could smell barbecue on the grill in the backyard, and bourbon, and the ever present smoke of their cigars lingering in the air. The smoke swirled lazily from their mouths and enveloped them in an acrid shroud, muffling their laughter—the sad, derisive laughter of middle-aged men.

I stood at the door, afraid to sit with them.

"Come here, boy," said my father, stretched out on a lounge chair with a drink in his hand. "Did you hear me?"

When I crossed the threshold, I could see my father's red, bulbous eyes, and smell his sweat. He was still wearing his post office uniform. Mr. Coltrane and Mr. Fry sat on either side of him, the weighty silence of their unfulfilled lives bearing down on me.

"Where's your brother?"

"In the basement."

"Go get him."

I have always been afraid of the basement in our old house, and it was no different in my dream: the pilot light of the furnace, the gray light shining through the gutter windows, the musty smell of earth. My brother Ralph lifted weights down there. I heard the sound of barbells hitting the concrete floor, but when I stopped halfway down the stairs to look for him, he was not there. I was sad that he wasn't there, and at a loss to explain my sorrow because I knew that he hated me.

Then the dream changed, and my father was standing in front of Ralph in the living room. Ralph, at fifteen or sixteen, two inches taller than he was, and growing.

"Who said you could wear my clothes?"

"Momma."

"My good shirt..."

"What, this thing?" Ralph said.

That riled him. "Let me tell you something, boy—you might wear my shirts, but you'll never be the man that I am!"

"I never want to be the man that you are!"

My father shot his large, calloused hand around Ralph's throat so quickly that I barely saw it. There was panic in my brother's eyes as he struggled to breathe. Fear. I woke up feeling uneasy about what I had dreamt, but not surprised. Ralph was missing again.

My brother had suffered from schizophrenia for most of his adult life, and occasionally would stop taking his meds. Why he'd stop taking them was beyond me, but when he did, his hotel room overlooking Turk Street would become too confining and he'd go days, even weeks, living on the streets.

I knew because sometimes I'd have to go looking for him.

It was early Saturday morning, not quite light outside, an unusual time for me to be out of bed in my cold apartment. I made some coffee, and listened to the news on National Public Radio: more US troops killed in Iraq, Afghanistan, and Pakistan. President Obama vows that America will continue to "fight for peace." Even though I had lived in my apartment in Presidio Heights for a little over a year, I still felt like an outsider in the neighborhood, and for good reason: there were very few black folks who lived there, and when I ran into them (the ones who were just scraping by like me), we looked at each other like we had just stolen one of massa's chickens—less interloper than outlaw who'd broken into the Man's henhouse. As for the other black people in the area, members of the upper class, they didn't look at me at all, or, if at all, only to make me aware that I was living there on the cheap and that they knew all about me nabbing one of massa's chickens.

I was living there because I had helped Judy and Michael find their son, who was strung out on crack. The Wongs had come to me through a mutual friend who knew that I wrote for a community newspaper in the Tenderloin. I found their son holed up with four other addicts in one of our more notorious dives downtown. The hotel, infested with bedbugs and other lower forms of life, would have made the crooks and robbers who founded our city proud.

They got their son out of there, scraping up enough money to send him to rehab. They mentioned, in passing, that they had purchased an old building on Sacramento Street, and had an apartment to let. They were generous with the rent, and didn't hassle me like some of my former landlords had.

I called Ralph's hotel room at eight—still no answer—and then the front desk. I had had numerous run-ins with Cheryl, the woman at the desk, and was in no mood to deal with her shit. I told her who I was, and asked her if she'd seen Ralph.

"I can't remember. This is a busy hotel, sir." She sounded exasperated by my question, angry even.

"Can I speak to Michelle, the social worker, please?"

San Francisco had turned many of the older hotels in the Tenderloin where Ralph lived into single room occupancy buildings, SROs, to house the homeless, with social workers and drug counselors working on-site to help them.

"Michelle isn't here yet," said Cheryl.

"Do you know when she's expected to come in this morning?"

She almost laughed at me. "I have no idea. I don't keep her schedule, sir."

I decided to wait an hour or so before I called again. To keep myself occupied I worked in the backyard garden downstairs. Before I moved into the apartment, there was no garden to speak of, the place was overgrown with crabgrass, oxalis, bindweed. When Judy showed me the yard, I asked her if I could pull the weeds out, try to grow a few things.

"You can do whatever you want," she said.

I bought a spade, a spading fork, shears, clippers, and a hand mower, and went to work, mainly on the weekends, clearing the weeds and tall grass, and discovering, to my surprise, a circular patio made of bricks in the middle of the yard. It was hard work pulling out the weeds between the bricks, but when I was finished, what a patio!

I weeded the flowerbeds that morning, but was too worried about my brother to enjoy the work. It was late autumn, and the weather was cool and damp and felt like it might rain, the first rain of the season. The dahlias and rose bushes had lost their bloom, but the French lavender still looked good. I was thinking about the planter boxes in the front of the building when I heard my telephone through the kitchen window. I stopped weeding and ran upstairs, hoping that it was Ralph. It was Michelle, the social worker.

"I haven't seen your brother in almost two weeks."

"Damn! I wonder where he could be this time?"

"Anywhere," she replied.

One of the many problems I always encountered when looking for my brother was that he really could be anywhere.

Arboreal Homicide

Shizue Seigel

It takes a long time to kill a tree. Not nearly as long as to grow it, of course, but still, taking down a seventy-foot-tall backyard tree without damaging any of the surrounding houses is a protracted and messy affair. When such a tree dies, there are few mourners and fewer witnesses. The Richmond District's streetscape is dominated by buildings jammed shoulder-to-shoulder two and three stories high, with hardly a bit of greenery to be seen. Even the postage stamp patches of lawn that used to adorn "front yards" a generation ago have been cemented over. Every kid who wasted his or her Saturdays manicuring these tiny, useless plots of grass must have grown up into a homeowner who paved over that grass the first chance he or she got. Those that did love gardening did not love their public gardens turned into doggie urinals. Today, the typical Richmond District street looks like a stucco desert, and only the residents with windows opening onto the backyards are privy to the captive green secreted at the heart of every block.

Dotted through neighborhood backyards used to be very large trees—mostly Monterey pines and cypress with a scattering of Norfolk pines and monkeypuzzle trees. The behemoth on my block had been planted as a seedling seventy years ago when the neighborhood was young. It matured into a substantial tree and then into a giant that dominated not only its own yard but the innards of a whole city block. Its sixty-foot-wide limbs shaded out all other vegetation in its shadow. Its crown stood thirty feet higher than the tallest buildings on the block.

To a bird winging from Golden Gate Park to the Presidio, the tree would have been one of a half-dozen along the way, poking green arbors above acres of asphalt roofing. Watching the birds that frequented the tree helped me see the city in a whole new way. Hawks perched on its highest limbs to scan for rodents and smaller birds. Ravens used it to look for carrion. Mourning doves nested there.

But my favorites were the mockingbirds. They used it to look for babes. I knew that spring was coming when they began to pour out their courtship songs from the top of the tree. They sang in shifts. One of my favorites arrived in May and sang every morning at 3:45 a.m. Another started his warbling at 7:20. There were others that staked out various daytime slots, but since they didn't wake me up, I didn't notice their schedules. The times did not vary from year to year, but the songs did. Did the same birds return year after year, or did they bequeath their locations and time slots to their offspring?

A single mockingbird can sound like a whole flock of birds because it imitates everything it hears, from the dry chuck-chuck of scrub jays to the liquid trills of songbirds. "Ooh, baby, come with me," the birdsong seemed to say. "Let me tell you about all the places I've been and the birds that I have known. I could tell you stories that would singe your pinfeathers." Sadly, some mockingbirds sang urban repertoires stitched together from cat howls and car alarms.

Beep-beep, buweep-weep, tock-tock-tock-tock. EEyoww!

Whatever they sang, the mockingbirds liked to perform from the top of the Monterey cypress because it was the tallest tree for blocks. They favored a bare branch near the tippy top because there was no foliage to obscure their courtship ritual. A bird would perch on the naked branch and sing its heart out for a few minutes. Then it would launch itself straight up into the air, spreading its tail and fluttering its wings to show off its distinctive black-and-white plumage. These musical performances would go on for hours. Sometimes two or three birds would vie for the same branch. As soon as one bird finished his song and flew straight up into the air, another mockingbird would scoot onto the branch while a third lurked nearby.

The tree signed its death warrant when it dropped a large branch onto the roof of a neighbor's shed during a rough winter storm. Nothing happened for several days, and then a crew of three arrived. They removed the fallen branch and stood around with the property owner and talked. The economically practical course would be to get rid of the tree, but I prayed that they were discussing how to prune the tree, something that had not been done for decades judging from the thicket of brushy side branches jutting from the trunk. Since the owner did not appear to use the yard for anything except tethering a German shepherd who barked from loneliness, I was not hopeful.

After several days, the two workmen returned with a block and tackle, which they hoisted up to a sturdy limb near the top of the tree. Then one of the men was winched into the tree, chainsaw in hand. I watched as he swung balletically around the tree, holding his body at a 45° angle and pushing off with strong legs against the trunk. Clearly he knew what he was doing. He secured branches with rope before turning on his saw. The cut branches were carefully lowered by rope to avoid damaging fences, roofs and surrounding vegetation. The whirr of the saw continued all day. I hoped that they were simply pruning, but by the next day, it was clear they were denuding the tree. I watched their progress from my office window. I was heartsick, but could not turn my eyes away.

After a couple of days, the top of the tree came down, and they began cutting into the four-foot diameter, limbless trunk. My stomach twisted when I saw the wood was a clear golden color, free of any streaks of dead grey. The trunk came apart as fat coins of wood, full of sap and vibrant shades of life and vitality. It took the workmen three days of steady work to kill the tree. I watched until nothing remained but the angry bee-buzz of chainsaws hacking downed limbs into bits small enough to carry out through the garage and toss into the wood chipper outside.

What would the mockingbirds do? The first couple of years, they tried to maintain their routines, returning in the spring to sing from rooftop stovepipes and air vents. But every year they started later in the spring and stopped sooner. By the third year, there was only silence. I can now see up the whole length of the block, and my window gets a lot of more sun, but nothing nudges me awake anymore at 3:45 a.m. to tell me, "Go back to sleep. Spring is coming, and all's right with the world."

Awful Sweet

Denise Sullivan

It's still a small Sunset house, the kind people once bought for thirty thousand dollars and it looks better today than it ever did then. I mean, it was what it was: purple or lavender, maybe fuchsia, as you liked to call the color that contrasted with your front yard flora, the bright hydrangeas, a few tea roses, and a sweet pink flowering bush common to the City we called "honeysuckle" because you could suck the honey right out of the stem.

The flagstone path never really fit in, like something out of Bedrock that belonged to the Flintstones, though later I learned it wasn't flagstone at all, just cement mid-century poured with a kidney shape scratched onto the surface. Eventually, it was painted brick red.

I would come to find we called just about everything by its wrong name back then. It was kind of a thing among San Franciscans, and we weren't the only ones with the habit. Our unique definitions and pronunciations were brought here by people like your family, migrants, farmers from the Central Valley – Tulare and Sacramenna as it's said – laborers, sailors, immigrants, the salt of the earth. I suppose they're how Valencia got to be "Valensha" and how Arguello and Cabrillo lost their "yos." Wrong is right when you're Californian by birth, San Franciscan by the grace of God, and granted special privileges by virtue of your nativity. Outsiders call us "provincial." I can't argue with them.

Your father came from Ireland, your brother had a brogue, but you, like me, were born here. And while we never got to the bottom of his waterfront tales, middleweight boxing career, and other opportunities missed when Sully left old New York, what came after is our story. Of course I'm as old or older than you were then, and so it is with some urgency I wish to document the acceleration of our expiration, the escalation of our cancellation, the physical deterioration, evaporation, and decimation of all that our kind deemed holy and good.

You see, there are no monuments, no statues, no hospital wings or streets with our names on them to remember us by. We've grown accustomed to disappearing without fanfare or a trace. Leaving no footprint, you might say we're impossibly green. And while some bodies will be returned for burial to Tallahassee or Omaha or Chippewa Falls, we remain, having conquered nothing, and heading for a grave in Colma or taking leave as ashes on the Bay.

It's been a stealthy but steady eradication, an economic process of necessary elimination, and it appears our kind is unlikely to survive San Francisco—though I hope you agree, it's probably for the best that we've arrived at the end of our line.

The house, though, still stands. Built in 1939, it's small but sturdy, the kind that people once happily paid thirty thousand dollars for so they could drink heavily and beat their children in the privacy of their own basement. I didn't know you all back then, I just heard tell. We never discussed the missing years, there was no need: you were nothing but kind – awful sweet – your old-fashioned term of endearment for me.

You once told me folk songs were your favorite but what you really loved were Tin Pan Alley hits, like the one about sweet little "Alice Blue Gown." The fog depressed you after all those years of coastal living and who could blame you? One summer we counted the days of sun (none) and that was enough for me, swearing to myself and others I'd never return. In your day, working people liked to leave and take sun at the River, in Sonoma, or in Los Gatos, as in one word, "Lascatos." These days, there's no need: the sun shines more often and burns dangerously hot in our backyards and, um, parklets.

You came from the era of the horse and buggy, the streetcar, the iceman, the raccoon coat, and the Model T, though in your sunset years, you were never one to resist the new. Remember the '60s and the hippies who lived in the Victorian neighborhoods and how they delighted you? The streets were teeming on our trip to Haight-Ashbury, and a teenager tripped out hard on your chartreuse scarf by Vera matched with a hot pink suit. We left the poster shop abruptly after that, and while you nervously laughed it off, I wonder now if the changes brought to the City frightened you. Was the arrival of the future a shock to you, too?

Stuck in the Avenues, occasionally left to an express ride downtown, in the '70s you made time with Mr. Coffee, endorsed by your friend, Joe DiMaggio. From Mayors Rossi to Willie Brown, this was your town: you knew your way around a Magnin store and banked with Hibernia until, well, you know.

In the '80s after the fall, you traded your walks, tailored skirts, and spectator pumps for leggings, ballerina flats, and a spot on the chesterfield. Fresh copies of *Vogue* and *Harper's Bazaar* fanned across the end table kept you stylish through the '90s when the nail color of the moment was that bloody black shade by Chanel they called "Vamp." You preferred yours frosted, or a nice mauve matte—always fresh, never chipped. You did your own, though your hair was left to

Romeo on Taraval. Eventually you whittled your closet down to just one final ensemble, a matching velour track suit with a sporty supportive shoe. Fueled by your faith and a little stubborn pride, once your sister died it was just me and you. We labeled your belongings, marking with sticky dots exactly what would go to whom. I have to say you timed your exit just right, before your neighborhood market was turned into a microbrewery.

You passed at the board and care named for St. Francis, though technically located in Daly City, sometime over a three-day weekend. The weekday staff called to tell me about it on a Tuesday, and just like that there was no one to call me "awful sweet" anymore. Sometime after the stroke and the recovery at Davies but before the funeral at Duggans and the final lunch at Westlake Joe's, the house was dismantled. The antiques and next-to-new treasures you collected from the consignment shops turned out to be junk, and I inherited your obsession with it (though I wrestled your monogrammed alligator suitcase from the slag heap of denial). Turns out there was a lien on the house on account of you having to put Sully into assisted living on 19th Avenue where it turns out he was having relations with another resident. Sadly, Dad was gone and unable to help navigate the indignities of your dotage. You told me there was no pain like a parent burying a child, and I believed you, though as an adult child charged with his cremains, I had the urge to argue.

And so the house still stands, undisrupted, for now. A bit on the small side for a modern family of four, its estimated value more than a million dollars according to a popular real estate app (don't ask). Painted a nice shade of orange, I think you'd call it "persimmon," the new owners have trained some crimson-colored bougainvillea to grow just under what was once your bedroom window. Sometimes I drive by and consider the above matters, a small effort to never forget you and the day–sunny, windy, no fog, not warm–as we prepared for the movies and what you liked to call the show. Sitting on the edge of your bed, anxious to catch the 48 or the 71 to the Alexandria, the Alhambra, the Northpoint, the Regency, the Parkside, the El Rey, the Bridge, the Royal, the Lumiere, the Surf, the Colosseum, the Coronet, the Cinema 21, who knows, I watched as you held your own gaze in the mirror, affixing those jet earrings, the difficult screw ons, and arranging yourself just so. Spritzing on your beloved Lily of the Valley, Chloé, or maybe Rive Gauche, your enthusiasm for readying yourself to leave the house spurred me to ask if ever you felt old.

"Oh, no, dear," you laughed, "I still feel just like a girl."

Your answer, like rays of sun returning to break through the seasonal gloom of the western neighborhoods, still cheers me.

Gold Underneath the Street

Lynell George

For months now, I've been at the time-bending task of emptying out my family home, breaking down history as if it were a set.

It's my childhood home, not the first, but the one we inhabited the longest. Moving through rooms, closets, and overstuffed drawers, I've unearthed all manner of lost treasures: pocket watches, maps, deeds to homes long razed. This house, I realize, became a nest–not just ours–but one made up of artifacts of generations of family members: Bibles and Sunday hats, old wallets still filled with gasoline "Charg-a-Plates" and oxidized pocket change, a cache of antique cameras still spooled with film, and a river of photographs documenting their journey west.

A few weeks back, making my way through the old kitchen, I put my hand in the dark recesses of a cabinet stacked with crystal water goblets, luncheon plates, and not one but two ornate turkey platters to find the most fragile porcelain teacup and saucer–once white with scalloped edges, a hand-painted small cluster of oranges at center. Beneath the fruit, in plainspoken yet fine brushstrokes, unscroll the letters C-A-L-I-F-O-R-N-I-A. Whose tiny cup was this? My grandmother's? My great aunt's? My mother's? Who purchased this souvenir? Who thought to save it? To protect it? I wondered. How had it survived so long, so dusty and delicate?

Loved ones brought home souvenirs like this almost translucent cup, to place on their shelves among their finest. To think that this memento perhaps made two journeys, from here to home and then here again. Was it a memento or a goal–or both?

Strange, it now seems in reflection, but my first understanding of California–the California of my mind–the one summoned most vividly in words, music, or visual artifacts–was the product of those who arrived from elsewhere. My African American forebears were pulled to this place by a myriad of desires–opportunity, weather, freedom, peace of mind. I lived in their myth. My maternal great aunt landed in Los Angeles to follow her Pullman Porter husband; her brother, my Uncle Harvey, also a Pullman man, headed north, to the Bay, dreaming of a quality of prosperity that eluded him in the South. My personal narrative of–and connection to–place begins with those circumstances that brought my family here; the inspiration–or kindling–was the California of their imagination.

I am a deeply-rooted Angeleno but I was pulled to San Francisco by my first glimpses. Those early impressionistic snapshots of the Bay came from visits to relatives' homes or our family-foursome's up-the-coast road trips. They also came from TV and books. Again, often an outsider's perspective–either a Quinn Martin police procedural of the '70s (*The Streets of San Francisco*) and, of course, much later the Beat Generation's rhapsodizing. The voices of Jack Kerouac, Allen Ginsberg, Lawrence Ferlinghetti, and Gregory Corso spun around my head–these bards of the new California, all transplants, too.

I was very late to Kerouac. By high school, I'd meandered

through *On the Road* and stalled... twice. But I'd been swept up by *The Subterraneans* (for which he swapped East Coast for West as the story's backdrop so that Paradise Alley became "Heavenly Lane") and then *Big Sur*–that rugged, unflinching coast that Kerouac described in such mournful detail, became rooted in my memory–became my own memories. The first drive I took north as an adult with a friend, in a convertible slithering up Highway 1, was about as mortifyingly cliché as it could come: My head full of a Massachusetts-born writer's descriptions and the tenor sax moods of a Pennsylvanian as my soundtrack–it effectively set up the scene. When we arrived at Nepenthe famished and ready for lunch, I paused to first take in that startling edge-of-the-Earth view. The universe seemed to know what I needed as confirmation: Stan "The Sound" Getz was drifting through an old bossa nova over the surround-sound stereo.

Securing an address and actually living in the Bay Area was an entirely different matter, of course; I'd moved to the outer Sunset which often only offered three hours of sun and a dedicated fog so thick and constant that at first I thought was rain. It was an adjustment for my Angeleno-being–an entirely different perspective of California, a bit more curated and consequently, manageable.

I didn't have a car for the first time since I'd earned my driver's license as a teenager. Moving about without one was both disorienting and liberating. I found my way by bus or on foot, learning the city step-by-step, stop-by-stop. San Francisco trained my eye in a different way. I'd grown up in a sunny place where often I moved past details at thirty, forty, fifty miles an hour. A scene or tableau that would come into focus for a moment and then move away from you, a streak of color and smear of sound. Here I could see things close-up. The crumbling Victorians; the noir tap rooms with their hints of dereliction or risk. Depending on the wind, I could catch scent of the sharp brininess of the Pacific, the blast of urine in BART stations, the aroma of scallions, garlic, and fish in late afternoons as I turned the corner in the Richmond.

In the years before corporate coffee was on every corner in the city, the ritual of the independent coffeehouse was already well established. Strong, heated, and often full-boil conversations about politics or city life were in animated display. The best ones were theater of their own. There was an urgency and liveliness, a particular sense of chance borne out of flow and accessibility that was, at the time, more difficult to come by in Los Angeles. One image that often returns: I had been making my way up a gentle incline in North Beach on Vallejo Street to stop in Caffe Trieste when the poet Gregory Corso thundered out of the front door and into the night, eyes blazing. I knew his face from the postcards in a rack at City Lights bookstore and the photo inserts of the books of the era I'd been living in; the face was just more anguished, the hair gray, wild like filament. When my friend arrived to join me at a small window table, I made mention that she'd missed him by mere minutes. A man seated next to us lifted a piece of paper–a stained napkin–with some ink pen scribblings: "He was just diagramming a poem. You want this?"

Oh, yes, I did. This was what I wanted–for a time: a textured life to press between pages of a book, one that looked becoming in black-and-white photographs. I wanted to live in a place that didn't just feel and look old, but protected its aged sacred places–the stories and characters that went along with them. What a city looked like, the noise and press and chaos of them, I finally began to put it together, was the patina of presence. It started with people: How they touched, shaped, and occupied space determined the nature of "home."

It's still about "space" to my mind. Not just measurable space–those miles demarcated in freeway exits–but the room to ask and play out that What If: Who might you be if you intersected with the place that might allow you to wander that question to its logical, meaningful end.

California, the best of it, is what lives and prospers in a liminal, unnamed space–somewhere between dreams, disappointments, and recalibration. It's harder to recognize, perhaps, because it's messy. It might look like defeat, or it might feel unfinished–or still in motion.

My San Francisco shuttle driver looked as if he'd stepped out of a '90s-era Hollywood adventure flick: barrel-chested, slicked-back hair, and ink-black wraparound shades. He was a man of few words–at first. Once he'd left off every fare but me, I noted a laminated placard, stuck in his cupholder: a Robert De Niro image from *Taxi Driver* and the words "Saint Travis" inscribed above it.

Even before this discovery, I was tipped off that he would be a necessary source to mine. Instead of zipping us through the usual downtown entryway streets, I looked up from checking messages to see that he was dragging us through the nether regions of the Tenderloin. Rows of blue tarp and trash-bag shanties and cardboard pallets lined the filthy sidewalks—hardly the exalted California Dream. I had to wonder: was this shortcut meant to warn, school, or discourage? We rode in conspicuous silence. Now, van emptied, I asked him about the placard.

He said it was a gift from his girlfriend. "All the cabbies and shuttle drivers have all these saints hanging from mirrors and knobs. I'm not religious, but she thought I needed some sort of saint."

"What did Saint Travis ward off?" I asked.

"It's just gotten so crazy," he speaks to me through the slash of rectangle of the rearview mirror, as we bump along toward my hotel in North Beach.

"The traffic?" I guessed.

"No, the people. I also drive a cab, and I just got off of a long shift and these assholes with the 'Take me to mumble mumble.' They don't know where they want to go. Or they're drunk. Or both.

Where doesn't seem to be important. Then, once we settle on a place for me to drop them, they jump out of the cab before the destination, without paying. Assholes. I took the keys and threw them at my boss—'NO MORE.' I mean, I've trained as a Navy SEAL. This shit is worse."

Place, of course, has changed too, certainly a reflection of the people who may not sweat certain details of destination. I could see it—or the absence of it—instantly: all this glass and steel and fewer tacky surfaces and the stories that go with them. I was struck by how much more like Los Angeles San Francisco appeared at first glimpse—South of Market particularly—with lofts and condos and sleek watering holes.

I met up with my friend Shelley, my old roommate from my grad school days there. I had merely a sketch of a plan. I wanted to locate what was still recognizable, what had stowed away. I wondered if that falling-down flat located off Divisadero where another friend once lived—with the warring turntables blasting punk and opera—still stood. Or if the bus still left you off in front of a vivid liquor store—always a story in motion.

Shelley and I retraced our old routes, the streets, ones closer to the ocean in the Outer Sunset. I still saw the shoulder-to-shoulder pastel houses but inevitably with a modernized, streamlined version interrupting the lines. In a certain way, visually, you could eavesdrop on conversations that were going on via architecture. I wondered how long this unusual mix of ragtag, working-class, aspirational, and DIY will be this way along the Great Highway.

On my final morning, we stop for coffee at Caffe Trieste, the same spot where I'd watched Gregory Corso fly out into the night. With a clutch of gray-haired men in hats and scarves lingering out front, it felt hearteningly unchanged. Protected, ducking in, I glimpsed a poster on the window. It took the wind out of me. Its dominant feature was a black-and-white image of a young Giovanni

'Papa Gianni' Giotta, Trieste's founder. The text advertised an upcoming memorial for Papa Gianni, that Saturday. I stood silently before the picture, looking at him behind the old counter opening day in 1956. A bar where I'd lined up weekends and evenings for a perfect cappuccino: "The first cappuccino bar on the West Coast!" as the family had long touted it. I had become enough of a regular that they'd remembered my order. For years, long after I moved away, I'd return, queue up, and watch the barista pull my espresso, place the brown cup and saucer before me. I didn't have to say a word. This, too, was home.

Even with all the buzz of gentrification that has restitched parts of North Beach, I was struck by how much of the feel—and stories—remained alive in the crevices of this place. This wasn't Italy; it was California as seen through the prism of his Italian youth. He was extending the line—possibility—himself with it. The cafe has been a meeting room for generations of artists, muckrakers, eccentrics, and tourists; but mostly, its role has been to lend support and succor to neighborhood, struggling, and/or working-class folks like Giotta, who himself had arrived from Italy with his family penniless and at loose ends. From a singing window-washer to a business owner, this cafe had saved him—and so many others. In certain ways, it is a monument to all of that—a sanctuary.

The sorrow I was feeling had settled somewhere deep. I was sorry I would miss the memorial, the arias that would be sung in his memory, the old neighborhood stories that would soar. Shelley and I lingered longer than we'd intended. I wanted to pause to take a few snapshots—details—to remember this moment, but I was at a loss. Not a cup or saucer. Not the jukebox full of arias. But what? We stopped next door at Trieste's adjacent storefront, their coffee-roasting business, and struck up a conversation with the man behind that counter. He directed our gaze toward the window, another poster of beloved Giovanni Giotta. The whole block, it seemed, was heavy in mourning. "There's a big thing this weekend," he told us, his body seemed limp with grief. Then he pushed two postcards—souvenirs—across the counter toward us: a blurred multiple exposure of the Caffe Trieste's interior—the roar of activity visible and Papa Gianni, a ghost, there again before me.

The man at the counter looked up over his glasses and into middle space, and then pronounced: "That's all we have left of poor Papa Gianni."

I don't want to believe him. I can't. Because what's circling around us—dusty and delicate but enduring—tells me something else: Papa Gianni is in these walls, in that jukebox. He's part of the feeling of that old North Beach. Those guys standing on the street corner, keeping the story moving, aloft; the woman with the kind smile who remembers your coffee; they'll be ghosts too, soon enough. But this old wooden monument of risk, big love, of life and acceptance is what we have left. How would I frame this shot? This feeling? Because it's quintessentially California. I realize now why it was so difficult to capture: because California moves through you. It is vigor and spirit. If we do it right, we leave our mark on hearts and in stories and souls.

If we're lucky, it's ongoing.

It's how we work with it.

The Poodle, the Refrigerator, and You

Don Skiles

The poodle, Alfie, had peed on the Sub-Zero refrigerator again. This was discovered when treading into the kitchen at 5:55 a.m. to make tea. It was dark now that early. Autumn, winter coming. That was certain. He would have to read Shelley's great ode with the line, "If Winter comes, can Spring be far behind?"

The North Koreans had successfully fired a missile capable of delivering a nuclear warhead on West Coast cities – Seattle, Portland, San Francisco – even Anchorage, Alaska. The German guy who'd only recently become a citizen (in the last month or so, that recent), whom he met regularly while walking Alfie — Alfie: a white miniature; a rescue; "100% poodle," the trusty old vet had proclaimed on examining him, after he was picked up in Palo Alto of all places; poodle heaven, although Carmel really was, having their annual Poodle Parade in early October when the town had so many poodles walking, strutting the streets in that crisp poodle strut, unmistakable, that he'd been stopped by an obviously baffled tourist, who had said, "Does everyone in this town own a poodle?"— yes, it was the German guy who'd claimed that a house on the corner of Lake and 28th was a "North Korean spy house. You see that large antenna? And they were flying the North Korean flag, I saw it. But they took it down." But who knew what the North Korean flag looked like?

The same man maintained several houses in the neighborhood were "birthing" houses. "The Chinese. They're brought here to give birth so the child is automatically an American citizen. Of course, if you watch closely, you can see young women going in. It's amazing what people don't know."

On YouTube, they showed the statue of the Unknown Surfer at the end of the municipal pier in Pismo Beach. Or maybe it was Hermosa Beach. There was also a commemorative statue of The Eagles's famous song on a corner in Winslow, Arizona, and one of Eadweard Muybridge, the real inventor of motion pictures, in the Presidio. Few people recognized his name, yet he had lived in San Francisco as a young man.

Why did Alfie pee on the Sub-Zero? From the sublime to the ridiculous. But he did. He did. As refrigerators go, the sleek, purring machine had cost a lot. It was worth it. But this said something, everything said something, about poodles. They were significant.

What was significant, daily, was that his wife was in treatment for ovarian cancer. So everything was noticed, examined, scanned, parsed. The language of oncologists could be almost mystical, like the great Avicenna or Boethius, whom he had actually read long ago in college. College! Had he not also read the Divine Doctor, Aquinas, and listened to his learned philosophy professor dispute? Occam's Razor! What a tool!

He wondered how many people knew what Occam's Razor was, or referred to? They all knew who the Pittsburgh Steelers were. There was a certain certainty there... "The knowledge of knowledge," Professor Passmore had said, looking out their tall classroom windows, which seemed, somehow, too tall. "Epistemology." At the very end of the semester, he had talked about Existentialism, and quoted Camus, "If only it could be said this is clear, then all would be saved."

At night, while he lay beside his wife who he hoped was sleeping soundly — he listened carefully — he heard the raccoons ascending and descending the big redwood tree right outside their bedroom window. It was not actually a tree, but a fern, a survivor from a long ago age of the planet, the Earth. With one of those "era" names. The raccoons had even peered into their bedroom from this tree, the cute masked faces, bright black eyes. Fierce enemies of dogs, though. And rightly so. The coon hunts of his boyhood, up on an Appalachian ridge, were the stuff of horror films. The terror the creatures must have felt. What was the point? He made sure not to let the poodle out then, although he clearly wanted to go. Maybe that was why he peed on the Sub-Zero.

One of the small bedroom windows showed the heavens, some stars, occasionally the mild shock of seeing the moon in one of its phases. Yeats had written a book about the phases of the moon. Arcane knowledge... One could lay and ponder, see the heavens wheel, although he knew next to nothing about the stars, constellations' names. A citizen of fifth century Athens knew much more than he did.

If he stayed awake, drifting in and out, checking his wife's now even breathing, outside it would gradually go grey, then lighten, with the coming of dawn. "Rosy-fingered Dawn" in *The Odyssey*. That would happen. And at about this hour, Alfie would jump down from the old bed and pad out the long apartment hall to the kitchen, to get a drink of water. Past the Sub-Zero. Another day beginning.

It might not happen... He could only hope. Another of those four-letter words.

The View From A Taxi

Kelly Dessaint

In my rickety National taxicab, heading back to the City on 280 from an airport run, I take the Sixth Street exit, which offers one of the best money shots of downtown San Francisco. I turn right onto Brannan to check out CalTrain, and think of my first encounter with this jagged city, spread out across the sky like a stately pleasure-dome. Hey, it's easy to feel nostalgic after making fifty bucks on one ride.

It was 1991. I was a ward of the state of Alabama. A welfare case. The old man was in prison, serving twenty years for child sexual abuse. Mom was back in Los Angeles. The social workers in the small town of Anniston had deemed her unfit on account of her being Californian. They locked up my kid brother in some Christian boys ranch. After an extended stay in an adolescent psych ward, some group shelters, and a couple of foster care homes, I ended up with a free ride to another state institution, the University of Alabama.

Even though I played the game, I was just waiting to get that diploma, rip it to shreds, and hit the road. As a trial run, during a summer break after my junior year, I traveled west of the Mississippi with my foster mother, whom I was also fucking. We backpacked up the Rockies through Santa Fe, Taos, Denver, and Boulder. Then west to Seattle, which was too grungy for me but she loved it there. I got mad and we fought all the way to Vancouver and back, then made up in Portland before driving down the Oregon coast to San Francisco.

From the moment I crossed the Golden Gate, it was love at first sight. While all the cities I visited had great bookstores, record shops, music scenes, art galleries and museums, none captured my imagination like the City by the Bay. Despite the poverty laid bare, the mentally ill wandering the streets, and litter floating in the wind, every day I stepped out of a cheap hotel on the edge of the Tenderloin and the sun cast a vibrant glow that made the urban detritus almost sparkle. At the top of each hill there was one discovery after another. In the afternoon, the fog rolled in and wrapped itself around the buildings like the smoke from a cigarette left smoldering in Sam Spade's ashtray. During the day, the sidewalks were crowded with fast-talking panhandlers, con men, freaks, and investment bankers. As shuttle buses jerked wildly up steep inclines, guys in leather bondage gear rubbed shoulders with elderly Asian women while making idle conversation with Midwestern tourists. The whole city felt Castro-adjacent, and walking down Haight Street to a chorus of "doses, doses" and "nugs, nugs" was almost as intoxicating as the drugs the hippie kids were peddling.

San Francisco was all I had hoped for: beautiful and tragic, a city of contradictions, where the weather suited my preferred attire of sport-coats and scarves. My foster mother hated every minute.

Two years later, I stepped off the Greyhound, a few hundred dollars in my pocket and a backpack with all my worldly possessions. My horoscope in the *SF Weekly* that day offered one word of advice:

Surrender.

For the next eight months, I stayed at the Green Tortoise hostel in North Beach rent-free, performing light housekeeping in exchange for a bunk. Too broke to take Muni without a discarded transfer, I spent my days wandering the neighborhoods of the City, mingling with the Beat ghosts in North Beach, loitering in the psychedelic revival of Haight Street, and killing time on the grass at Buena Vista Park or the Panhandle until the fog rolled in. Some days I'd sit on a bench at the park on top of Russian Hill and just watch the light change as the sun moved across the sky.

I was reveling in a dream, but in reality, I was devastated. My foster mother had finally left her husband. For a French exchange student. Already, a traumatic childhood hung around my neck like an albatross. This betrayal was like a curse. No matter how bad things got, though, San Francisco was outside waiting for me, the air itself a comforting embrace.

Eventually, the new manager at the Tortoise threw me out for selling acid to the foreign backpackers. With nowhere else to go, I rode the 38 Geary bus, back and forth, from Market Street to the beach, until the sun came up, when the realization that my San Francisco days were over finally registered. It was time to crawl back to my mother's garage in Los Angeles, the only place left for me to go and regroup.

Since the Grateful Dead were playing the Oakland Coliseum that weekend, it wasn't hard to find a ride. For three nights I slept in some Deadhead's van with his dogs in the parking lot of a Holiday Inn before finally heading south.

Over the next two decades, my desire to move back to the Bay never wavered. During the late '90s dot-com boom, when most new residents looked like they'd just stepped out of a window display at The Gap, the prospect was grim. After the bust, a small window of opportunity opened, albeit briefly. In 2009, shortly after we got married, Irina and I talked about leaving LA. She shared my love of the Bay. We found a cheap studio in Noe Valley, but just as we were about to quit our jobs, she got promoted. They offered her the kind of money you didn't turn down at the height of a recession. So we rented a loft in the Historic Core, blew a bunch of money on tattoos and tattoo removal, built an impressive record collection and, every few months, drove up the coast.

Four years later, when Irina was laid off, we immediately started looking for a place in San Francisco. Based on Craigslist ads, median rents at the time were already around $3000 for a one-bedroom in the deep Sunset. Tiny studios in the Tenderloin were going for $1800. It was obvious we couldn't afford anything in the City. We ended up across the bay in Oakland's Temescal.

While the Town offers a sense of stability, driving a cab in the City keeps me allied to the place where I first staked a claim. At first I did the Uber/Lyft thing before quickly realizing that using your personal car as a cut-rate taxi isn't sustainable and the "sharing economy" that fuels the latest tech boom is just a predatory business model designed to push workers' rights back to the 19th century.

I loved driving in San Francisco though, constantly exploring and figuring out the lay of the land, learning hotspots and landmarks, the history and lore, as well as having an insight into the collective consciousness of a boomtown in full boom. So I signed up for cab school and became a bonafide taxi driver.

Now I feel more connected to the City. For better and worse. There is still an exhilarating madness that permeates the streets, a reminder of what makes this place so unique, but it's fleeting amid the growing desperation and brazen poverty that's impossible to ignore. San Francisco has never been a place to stumble, much less fall.

Like so many other Bay Area residents, new and old, Irina and I were barely scraping by as rents and the cost of living skyrocketed.

What she earned as a freelance designer and my taxi wages paid the bills, but not much else. Still, we survived for three years. Then Irina left. Then she came back. Then she got pregnant. For the next seven months we didn't talk about what it meant to bring a child into an already untenable situation. This is what we wanted. The Fates be damned.

On January 5th, we set up camp at Alta Bates Hospital in Berkeley to wait for the birth of our daughter, who arrived, reluctantly, three days later. Weighing in at eight pounds, twelve ounces, with a head of dark hair just like her mother and inquisitive eyes that darted around the room, her first bewildered take on the world was akin to my own: WHAT THE FUCK? WHAT THE FUCK? WHAT THE FUCK? As she looked at me for answers, I could only sob in ecstatic wonder. At this moment, the little creature in my arms was the only thing that mattered.

Despite a complicated labor that left the hospital room looking like a murder scene, the joyous surge of pride at seeing my daughter born was a very real reminder that life is full of twists and turns. While filling out the birth certificate, the nurse asked my profession. I paused and thought of the birth certificates of the fathers that came before me: My paternal grandfather was a general laborer. My mom's dad, a miner. My old man was listed as a clerk, even though he was in the Army.

"Writer," I told her.

Sure, it's a full-time gig that pays slave wages – barely enough to support a geriatric cat, much less a growing child – but would it have been more honest to say "taxi driver"? If I were to say that, most people would respond, "You mean, like Uber?"

No, not like Uber. I drive a cab in San Francisco, which, up until a few years ago, was a legitimate blue-collar job, in a city where blue-collar jobs used to mean something. The taxi industry is full of men and women who've raised both daughters and sons in the City, who've provided for their families, bought houses, traveled, paid for college and medical expenses, and still do, as taxi drivers. It's next to impossible to imagine now that the profession has been diluted by eggheads in tech who believe robots can do any job better, and the Millennials who bemoan the lack of decent jobs and yet celebrate the systematic dismantling of one decent job after another in their constant pursuit of convenience. Which is why I thank the stars my daughter was born under Obama's administration, so we were covered for maternity care through the Affordable Care Act. Otherwise, what? Google how to give a DIY caesarean birth?

After the nurses yanked my little girl away, they washed her hair and gave her some vaccinations. When Irina and I asked, out of curiosity, why they give newborns so many shots, the nurses told us that for some babies, this is the last time they receive medical care, unless it's an emergency. That made me think long and hard about what it means to be a parent. Yeah, it's hard not to worry about providing for my child. And as someone trying to make money in an industry that's being attacked by unscrupulous companies that eschew regulation through semantics, it's hard not to freak the fuck out. But I think of my laborer grandfather, who was essentially a drunk; my miner grandfather, who, after contracting black lung, tried his luck at farming before moving to Southern California to be a janitor; and my dad, who sacrificed his true identity as a gay man to raise a bunch of kids, ultimately ruining his life, my mother's life, and severely fucking up the lives of five children – if not more. I'd rather my daughter see me as someone who followed ideals, however foolhardy, than someone who surrendered to a distorted concept of what it means to be middle class. Or a taxi driver…

After fighting traffic onto Townsend, I pull into the CalTrain taxi stand. There are six cabs lined up already, leaving me plenty of time to smoke a cigarette and ruminate a little more before the train pulls into the station. Of course, the same old fear lingers, that I'm just one misstep from ending up in some guy's van again. Or worse: living in a broken down taxicab in Upton Alley. But at least my daughter was born in Berkeley. And to the best of my ability, she'll grow up in the Bay Area. I'll try not to cringe when she comes home from school one day saying "hella this" and "hella that." Or starts rooting for the Giants. And who knows, some day we might still make it to San Francisco... One can always dream.

In the distance, the clanging of the train gets closer. I pitch my cigarette butt and get back in my taxi to find out what's waiting for me at the front of this line.

Eras, Areas, and Unruly Errors

Barbara Stauffacher Solomon

Through lots of eras and over lots of areas, I broke lots of rules. Now I wonder if it was a good idea?

It's 2017 and I'm home in San Francisco. Every morning, I hit a phone app and a driver arrives, smiling, to drive me to the pool in the Presidio to swim laps. Lyft drivers are unfailingly friendly. We use first names immediately. The driver begins telling me his or her life story, and asking me mine, as they tell me to fasten my seat belt.

"Where are you from? How long have you lived here? You were born here? Your father and mother, too? Amazing."

It is as if drivers are vetted for their passion to make conversation as well as drive. We turn from my house toward the bay to Bay Street, continue west on Marina Boulevard, go past the Marina Green, and turn left to the pool in the Presidio. After I swim laps, back and forth, back and forth, I hit the app again. Another driver arrives, smiling.

"I live in Sacramento, but I like to drive in San Francisco," she says as she turns right onto Marina Boulevard.

"I used to teach English," she says on Bay Street.

"But I make more money driving here," she says, turning right at Columbus.

"It helps to support my kids," she says as she makes a left on Francisco into North Beach.

Last week on my ride home, my fellow passenger (share the ride, pay half price) was a young woman with long brown hair, bright eyes, degrees in chemistry and economics, and lots of I'm-new-to-town questions:

"What's the best part of town to see?" she asked.

"Here," I answered. "You're riding through it. Look, there's the Golden Gate Bridge, the Bay and the sailboats, Alcatraz, Sausalito, Mt. Tamalpais, the fog, and the sky. Look the other way. That's the Marina District. There's the Palace of Fine Arts, a survivor of the 1915 Fair. A block up on Divisadero is where I lived until I was 17. Across the street is where Marilyn Monroe lived when she was married to Joe DiMaggio."

"Are there any great buildings in San Francisco?" she asked.

"There is one, two blocks from here, on Jefferson Street; a steel-and-glass hunk of architecture that European exile architect Richard Neutra introduced into the otherwise wood-and-plaster façades of the Marina."

She googled it. "It's now selling for $3.95 million."

"Everything is these days. Even the old Victorians."

"You don't like Victorians?"

"Too cutesy-pie for me. I like minimalism."

"Oh?"

"I'm a Modernist."

"What's a Modernist?"

"For someone my age it seems impossible you never heard of

Modernism."

"I'll google 'Modernism.' "

Driving down Bay Street, we passed Galileo High School (where I went), Ghirardelli Square (where I created the signage and two walls of supergraphics), the Dolphin Club (from which I swam in the Bay), and Fisherman's Wharf (where I danced a gig in the Copacabana). The driver turned right on Stockton Street and I'm home. We three said goodbye, almost hugging each other but not quite.

I'm always happy to get home. I walk up two flights of stairs and open the door and all the windows I can reach; then up another flight of stairs to open the door to the roof deck. The four by four inch white painted beams sit on regularly spaced white four by four inch by eight-foot posts, columns enclosing an outdoor room with dining table and chairs. When my husband Dan Solomon, daughter Nellie, and I moved here in 1972, all the North Beach rooftops had these post-and-beam structures to hold up clotheslines. Every Monday morning, the Italian ladies climbed up their back stairs carrying baskets of sweet smelling wash to hang on the lines. The steaming sheets, blowing in the wind, looked like the white sails of the sailboats down the block. Now the ladies have washer-dryers in their basements here or in the Marina. Now the rooftop pigeons own the views of the Bay, Russian Hill, Nob Hill, Telegraph Hill, and the sky.

San Francisco is surrounded by water on three sides, mountains on the other. The area was mostly sand dunes until the 1849 Gold Rush, when ambitious new-money miners needed an instant city; a place to build mansions, saloons, and an opera house. The yellow hills and dales where cows grazed were covered with straight lines of streets, down and up, down and up, east to west, north to south, to make a gilded paradise, a gridded city.

Initially, the Marina District was seen as a tabula rasa; tidal land invisible except to sea birds and fishermen, a piece of white paper waiting to have lines drawn on it. Then it was landfill, a place to dump ruins and rubble resulting from the 1906 earthquake and fire. Next, it was a (popular, according to my mother) seaside amusement park during the phoenix-rising-from-the-ashes Panama Pacific International Exposition. It was developed in the '20s as an advantageous place for bay view taxable property, valuable real estate.

The Marina District wasn't built to look modern, just new, desirable, and eminently respectable. These houses were originally bought mostly by Italians flourishing in North Beach, successful but anxious to move up and out to the Marina. Located between Bernard Maybeck's orange Palace of Fine Arts, the blue bay, and green hill of Fort Mason, the Marina looked like a nostalgic Italian's idea of a new-world Italy. They planted large backyards with fruit trees, zucchini, artichokes, and tomatoes. Plaster facades were painted, not bright white like most tongue and groove wooden San Francisco flats, but pussy pink, orange sherbet, and strawberry cream, ornamented with a plethora of nostalgic decorations: Palladian arch windows, plaster angels and arches, balconies and balustrades, garlands and brackets, porticos, moldings, vases, and volutes. Even now, especially now, lots of the young techies pay exorbitant rents to get flats in the Marina, to jog along the Marina Green, to walk to sailboats moored at the yacht harbor, to bike across the Golden Gate, or to sit on Chestnut Street or Union Street in shorts at outdoor cafes eating pizza, drinking cappuccino, and texting emojis rather than bothering to spell words. And though the grids are always visible, no one notices them.

It's another morning in San Francisco and again I'm asking the Lyft driver, "Do you know anything about Modernism?"

"No, what's that?" he says. "I'm from Kazakhstan."

The next morning I asked the Lyft driver, a smiling young man with a black beard, "Do you know anything about Modernism?"

"I'm from Brazil. I've been to Brasilia. That's all the Modern stuff I want to see," he said.

"Why did you leave Brazil?" I asked.

"There's too much corruption there now. I couldn't live with it any longer. I love being a Lyft driver. I love this drive from North Beach to the Presidio. I love San Francisco."

Then the next morning I asked my Lyft driver, a talkative redhead with glasses, "Do you know anything about Modernism?"

"Isn't that something that happened in the '60s?"

"No. But, well, kinda. Both eras were about young people doing their own thing, but the Modern movement was about making new rules whereas the '60s were about making no rules, about breaking rules."

I had meant another kind of modern; the Modern Movement as people meant it in Europe in the experimental '20s and '30s, rebellion against the rules of the past. The Modern Movement that had disobeyed all the old rules blindly, and then, proceeded to obey all their new rules blindly.

California, at least in the '60s, was where no one seemed to use words like "rules" and "obey." Fun had been invented in California. Let It All Hang Out. We have fun being free. Supposedly. Free to raise hell. Free to go to hell. In California, we are free do anything we want to do, but usually, we don't know what we are supposed to do, and certainly we don't know what we want to do. There were no rules in California so I went to Basel to learn some. My husband Frank Stauffacher had just died in San Francisco and I was lost. In 1956, people didn't mourn. They put on a tough front, talked hard, and smoked lots of cigarettes. I fled to where I could learn to be a designer in order to support myself, and my young daughter Chloe.

Good Design implied good intentions, good solutions, the good life, and good paychecks.

Basel didn't have many gridded streets but there were lots of guiding rules and everybody seemed to obey them. (It was only after living in Switzerland for years that I understood why the Swiss drank so much and traveled to exotic lands so often and behaved so violently at Fasnacht.) Switzerland was a good place to study design: good design on the outside, lots of beer and bratwurst inside. In Basel, I learned that design is a cover.

"Learn some rules," Armin said. "Follow them. Later, if you are brilliant enough, you can break all the rules. Until then you can hang onto them." Swiss graphics has always been based on lots of rules.

My teachers Armin Hofmann and Emil Ruder knew them and patiently taught them. Step-by-step. Day-by-day. The Modernism Movement was going to save the world. And me. I was delighted to have some rules to follow but no matter how much I tried to dress Swiss, and act like a good Swiss frau, I was a stranger from another land, that bleached-blond-American-woman, twenty-six and good looking. Fine. No one knew me. No one saw a young widow.

"Make a clear solution," said Armin. "There must be no confusion."

The God of the Modern Movement smiled down on rational thinking, clear forms, pure colors, and clean black-and-white solutions. The simple is not simplistic. Ornament is a Crime. No more hypocrisy. No more affectation, dishonesty, deceit, dissimulation, and duplicity. No more serifs: we used sans serif Helvetica. No phony words, no propaganda. Print clear facts on a clean piece of white paper. No more decorated palaces and cathedrals to overpower the people. No more intimidating museums: Show paintings on the streets, in brightly lit temporary tents. No more moldings: Design clean white walls for everyman to have. Give us sun, light, and air. Devise pure and beautiful tools, chairs and tables, pots and pans and buildings. Indeed, everything became so clean it disappeared.

People got bored. No one was having fun. Instead of Kennedy, we had Nixon.

"Let's go to the movies." "Viva Las Vegas." "Pass me a joint." "Give me a hit." "Greed is good." Unintended consequences prevailed. Unruly rules pervaded. Only the rich bought into the Modern Movement. Only the rich could afford those carefully sculpted chairs and glass skyscrapers. Good Design — intended to bring good products to the people — became capitalist symbols of power. An example: the Walker Art Center's recent publication *Hippie Modernism/The Struggle for Utopia,* a catalog for an exhibition, which speculates about the '60s. Included are issues of *Scanlan's,* a political magazine published in 1970-71. Muckraker newspaperman Warren Hinckle was the editor; I was the art director. What is written is very complimentary, but seen, not from 1970, but from 2017: The use of Helvetica in support of counterculture ideas was a subversive use of a typeface that has already become closely identified with corporate communication of the era... modernist typography is recuperated from its tight identification with corporate capital, and rehabilitated to express reform... Wrong. I am old. I always used Helvetica because I always used Helvetica; they are so young, they only thought of Helvetica as spelling out corporate propaganda. We met recently when the exhibition came to the Berkeley Art Museum and Pacific Film Archive. We talk about everybody getting everything wrong and laugh.

I'm jumping around too much; going back-and-forth between Modernism as the type of honesty and a type for hypocrisy, Basel and San Francisco, 1962 and 2017, but that is the way it was. In 1962, John Kennedy said to everyone, "The greater our knowledge increases, the greater our ignorance unfolds," and Armin said to me,

"Now you know enough to be a designer." I put together a portfolio of my Swiss work and opened a design office in San Francisco. Oblivious to future loop-the-loop rides and Helvetica falls, I was delighted to work with Modernist architects doing work for rich clients. Back in San Francisco, I learned to use design as my cover.

It was wonderful to get off the plane and smell the salt air of the Pacific. I joined the Dolphin Club and swam in the salt water every morning. I made money and bought a white Fiat convertible. I rented an apartment in Tiburon so Chloe could have eight cats and walk to school across the street. I was young and beautiful. Everybody was. And we thought it would last forever.

In the '60s, everything was booming. Everybody was building New Towns (like the Sea Ranch was meant to be) and suburbs (like those that became Silicon Valley.) I worked like a machine designing signs, brochures, and logos. Painting clean forms in clear colors, plus black, on white white walls, big and without content. Progressive Architecture called them "supergraphics" and put them on their cover.

In the '90s, I started to draw, type, collage, and cut and paste "Plays on a Page" on 8-1/2 x 11 pieces of paper. They are small areas with all the content I can fit within my grid on the page.

The era is now the 21st century. The area is everywhere and nowhere. No one knows if errors are errors or alternate games with new or no rules. Rules change every second and everyone disobeys them blindly.

No need for Modernism. Everything is more modern than the Modern Movement could have hoped for. No one (except me maybe) is still hooked on the looks of books. No need for big impressive hunks of architecture. All the words are hot air in the clouds. Now everything everybody needs to know is up there somewhere in superclouds, and at the same time, miniaturized in smartphones in our pockets. The smartphone is the great equalizer. If it's not on TV or our smartphone, it didn't happen. We may not be smart but our smartphone is.

It's ok. The sun is out in San Francisco. The seagulls dive over my deck and the pigeons still coo sitting on the hot water pipes. I'm old and okay, with a credit card and a smartphone in my cargo pants pocket. Every morning, I hit the app on my smartphone and a friendly face will arrive to drive me to the swimming pool to swim laps, back-and-forth, back-and-forth.

Out in the Excelsior

Alice Elizabeth Rogoff

"There's a customer of mine named Hines who wants his house sat," said Michael Katz, the bike store proprietor. "And he'll pay per day and all you have to do is sit there, never go out, keep the shades down, and watch the house."

"That's all?" asked Deborah.

"Oh, yeah," said Mike. "There's one more thing. You have to feed the guy's dogs."

Hines was terribly afraid of having his things stolen. He had been robbed three times, and the third time, he'd been so enraged that he'd run out of his house with a loaded gun raised over his head, his angry words no language for a delicate girl's ears. By the time his neighbors had calmed down and gone back to tending their Sunday hedges, Hines was pacing up and down, back and forth, worrying every ounce of worry out of him, wishing that he didn't have to go to work every morning, trying to think of a way to protect his things, of which he had many.

Hines's house was filled with the most incredible variety of old magazines, newspaper clippings, half-eaten food, broken tools, and two large Boxers which he kept in the basement – except for the moments when he let them run free, and they, not appearing to be dissatisfied with their lot in life, came charging out, leaping on him, and licking him wet with their adoring tongues.

"It's the dogs I really worry about," Hines said to Deborah. "I don't know what I'd do if someone took my dogs." Deborah stood in the doorway, a bus transfer still in her hand, trying to peer past Hines into the pink stucco house, which if Hines hadn't lived there, would probably look and feel like any other working class house in a working class district of San Francisco.

As it was, though, there was no spot in that structure where one could sit and feel comfortable, and one always needed to move, hoping that it was just this chair or that sofa, but really knowing that it was the air, that it was everything about the place. It made you feel like you had to keep looking over your shoulder.

"And another thing," Hines continued, "I'll call every few hours to make sure you're still here."

Hines, Deborah noticed, had the nervousness of a gopher, a characteristic oddly contradictory with his six foot three football player appearance, his short dark hair sticking to his head like nails.

It was a hard house to house sit. Deborah wandered from room to room, eyeing the collected debris, wondering if anything was really valuable, stepping over pages and pages of old catalogues, of flyers advertising supermarket sales, of instructions on how to use a power saw. The papers rolled off the shelves, overflowing onto the floor, piling in floods of dust. She tried to dance, she tried to read, anything to keep busy, she thought, but there was nothing to do, because in that house it was difficult to do anything. She simply sat by the phone, waiting for it to ring, staring at the thick beige drapes that had to be kept closed. Anything, she thought, to keep from going crazy.

And then, she knew what to do. She knew that there was one sane thing that sane people could do in that house. She knew that Hines's house needed mad poetry like a mirror needs glass.

"Hugh?" Deborah said. "Alice? Come visit, and bring all your mad poetry with you."

Do you know what mad poetry is? It's the poetry you write when you're lonely, when you're sad, when you're crazy, when your only lover decides he doesn't like you, when lights go out for no reason, when the colors of your hands are more intense.

And you read mad poetry when it's right to read mad poetry, when it creeps out of drawers and sealed envelopes that say "Do not open for five years" and when you need something to share and laugh about, when you know who your friends are and you need someone to say, "That's not mad, that's only lonely."

An orgy of mad poetry in Hines's house. Hour after hour of cracked glass, of broken stars, of terrible awful poetry written on napkin scraps.

"That's not mad," we hugged each other. "That's only lonely."

And after we left, Deborah went back one more day. And the papers were no longer strange, the dogs were no longer strange, the house had a purpose. And that's when Deborah knew it was time to go. And we watched birds, and flew kites, and loved each other, and tried to live as sanely as we could.

Learning to Breathe with Sea-Lungs

Stefanie Doucette

"Whoa, you have less stuff than I do and I live in an RV." Kay and I stand on the sidewalk in front of my new apartment in the Avenues, staring at the open, gaping mouth of my trunk. I'm not surprised when her shock at its relative emptiness gushes out, as the trunk yawns and pops open, revealing my life to the world. Piled together, it really does look pretty puny with the sun thrown on it like that.

The way the sun shines on this coast, in this corner of the west, still makes me uneasy sometimes. You'd think after almost two years I would have come to welcome it by now, but no. It's not a bright, blaring sun. Or a weak, hazy underdog sun. It's a take-it-or-leave-it, bright but not too bright sunshine. The kind that streams in through an elderly aunt's dusty window panes at 3 p.m. as she's telling you stories of the life she used to live. It makes me anxious, because you can't hide or distract yourself from anything in a sun like that.

"I'd have less if it weren't for all my books. They really get in the way of my minimalism." I say this like an Olympic marathon winner talking about needing to improve the time on his final lap; my maniacal obsession with keeping the material aspect of my life as limited as possible coming across as humility in the moment, and not the defense mechanism it actually is.

Like a fugitive of sorts, I like to keep my life as transferable at a moment's notice as possible. You know, should I ever have to flee in the middle of the night. Not that I ever would, I just prefer to keep my options open.

"Well, you really didn't need my help moving in, did you?" Kay says, a smirk crossing her usually iron-stern face. It's true. I had very little need of her help. I just loved being around her. Like a little girl with her young, attractive stepmother, I craved her attention and yearned to "grow up" to be her in a sense, even though she was really only a year or two older than me.

"Oh, c'mon. You and Em were just parked right around the corner anyways. Plus, I'm letting you keep your shit here while you're gone, remember?" I smirk back, to let her know I actually did really appreciate her help. It just felt wrong moving in all by myself. My new roommates were all out of town.

Not that I hadn't moved myself into and out of what felt like thousands of apartments over the past few years – always solo, usually in the mid-afternoon. I liked to move in when the house was silent and not being used by anyone else, all at work or school or whatever other occupation kept them away, so I could explore it in peace: peek into kitchen cabinets, open bathroom drawers, flick the stove on and off just to assure myself it worked, and that I was really rooted there in the moment and not just conjuring up yet another new place. That's the problem with moving around like a nomad—it starts to not feel real any more. It had started to just pour over me like a breeze until, poof!, I'm on to the next home with all new cabinets and drawers and stoves to explore. I relied on any little thing, like a quick whiff of heat from a kitchen appliance, to make it seem concrete and real.

There was the place in Boston, with all its flamboyant hats (red, yellow, purple, blue) spilling out of every orifice, the carcass remains of the life of Fumi, a transgender woman whose name was still on the lease for the attic space even though she had been deported almost four years earlier. There was the basement in Cedar Rapids, where I shared an air mattress for three months. Then Vermont, LA, Sacramento, Berkeley, Oakland, Berkeley again. Variations of those thousands of Craigslist sublets in between that all blurred together in my mind.

But this place was different. On the corner of 22nd and Fulton, it was untouched, empty, blank. Nothing in the cabinets and the drawers yet. Believe me, I looked. And I still did check the stove when we walked in, too, first thing after setting down everything I owned (and had carried with me over the past several years of traveling) on the worn hardwood floors. They were the type of floors that cradle the dirt and grime of a hundred-plus years in between their cracks, that constantly uproots and shifts around when you walk on them, meaning constant sweeping. My mother's house back east, off Old Boston Road, had floorboards like that, too.

"Alright, there it is," I said to Kay with my hands on my hips, sizing up everything laid out in front of me: a trash bag filled with pillows and blankets; the suitcase I had flown to California with two years before, leaving all my bulky woolen sweaters behind because it wasn't big enough, and I refused to pay the airline's fee for a second bag; one box with picture frames, some old undeveloped Kodak cameras, colored pencils, and whatnot; and of course a big old duffel full of books, always the hardest piece to lug. In the corner, a mattress I had bought on Craigslist from some techies in SoMa who were getting rid of a spare unused bed set for $50. They hadn't known how to tie it onto the roof of a car, and I still like thinking of their confused faces trying to figure out the instructions to a pack of straps I had bought at Home Depot.

Kay digs through one of her own suitcase that she brought with her and hands me a book. *The Days of Abandonment* by Elena Ferrante. Kay claims she's the new Sylvia Plath.

"Feel free to go through any of my books," she says, kicking the purple suitcase closest to her left foot. "Enjoy them. Thought you might like this one, though. Read it. Let me know what you think."

I flip it over and scan the back. It's about a woman in a city she never loved, who finds herself clueless as to how to root her life after the husband who brought her there leaves her. She's a woman whose world is all of a sudden different, in a place she needs to figure out how to understand, in the absence of help and that someone who left her to her own devices. A woman a lot like me.

On Monday, after a music festival in Golden Gate Park, Kay and her girlfriend Em are leaving town. Packing up their RV, traveling around the country. Their plans are vague: a brief stint in Joshua Tree; Texas for the holidays with Em's family. Beyond that, not much else to go on, except that they've been here for a decade and are feeling antsy to leave and see if they can make it somewhere else.

"We'll be back this time next year," Em tells me later that afternoon, making a swooping motion with her arm at the scene unfolding around us. Like they're Santa Claus or something, and I'm a child who will spend the next twelve months knowing them in terms of our short time together, and anticipating their return with almost desperation. Their presence is really their absence, and the anticipation of the thrill that their return will bring. The only difference is Santa Claus always returns. With an address attached to wheels and no hard and fast trajectory, Kay and Em are leaving me with no such reassurance.

And still like the child, I fall asleep that night, on my perch in an apartment a block and a half from the Park, listening to M. Ward play his set to a roaring crowd right outside my window, comforted by the thought that my friends' voices are mixed in with those notes floating up to me. All the cheap beer and the sun had hit me with a little melancholy wooziness, so I had decided to head home a little early, leaving them there, sad to miss out, but also feeling the happiness of living close by the Park for the first time.

M. Ward sings some questions to the crowd:

And I said,
What do you do with the pieces of a broken heart?
And how can a man like me remain in the light?
And if life is really as short as they say
Then why is the night so long?

And I lay there, in the deepening early-evening dark, with unpacked boxes piled all around me – the collective lives of me, Kay, and Em, each coming and going in our own way.

"How long have you been here?"

It's hard to say.

"Why did you move here?"

I don't really know.

I'm pretty awful at these conversations. First dates, interviews. And generally most interactions that happen when you're the new bartender at the local bar with a group of grizzled regulars who remember when the beer was $2 a pint, not $4.

Andrew's one of those regulars. A few years back, he discovered it when he lived in the basement art co-op next door, because no one ever really seeks these kinds of spaces out. More like they roll in like the fog, settle around the architecture, and leave their imprint in the walls, the chairs, the steam-spotted glasses. He's a filmmaker, because everyone there has their own unique hustle.

I get the feeling that he wasn't asking me these questions, these low-key infatuated inquiries, because he's particularly taken with me. It's just that I'm new, and he's lived on this block for so many years. New things rarely happen at this kind of place, which was part of its appeal, really. In a city famous for new things popping up too quickly and aggressively, spending every evening in a bar that still plays music out of a dusty Sylvania stereo from 1995 is a comfort for those who have been there since before all that "development."

"Did you do something different with your hair? I like it."

Oh, god. I pretend to be busy restocking lemon wages, and run off, mumbling about needing to get more from the walk-in out back.

But Andrew keeps coming back, not every night like some of the regulars, whom you can set both your watch and the temperature of your kegs by, but about once a week or so, when he's not traveling to LA for a shoot, or in a rabbit hole with his on again-off again girlfriend whom I've never seen, only heard stories about. We stop talking about my hair and why I moved to San Francisco, and start talking about other things: friends' deaths, trips home, being an artist in a city that's turning its back on them.

We start sharing joints together on slow nights, beers when I stop by on my off nights. I start looking forward to seeing his curly shoulder-length ponytail go bobbing past the window, knowing it means in a moment he'll be turning the doorknob and joining the crowd for the evening.

One night he stays too long, has a few too many beers. I let him linger while I count the money, restock the pint glasses, lock up. Everyone else is gone by now, moving on to continue drinking on their front steps, or at other bars still open down the road.

We both seem to know we'll be heading out together. Unspoken, it seems like after so many months it's finally the right time for that. And for the first time, instead of heading in separate ways at the curb of that Divisadero corner – me toward the bus, and Andrew up the hill home – we start walking in the same direction together, naturally, no questions asked. With my hands tucked in his coat pockets, we spend twenty minutes waiting for the bus, the 5R heading down Fulton, and then decide to just walk instead. It's only about half a mile or so, and we're both a little drunk still anyhow.

But when we climb the hill, the fog comes pouring over us at the peak, thrilled like an animal left alone to finally have someone to dampen at this time of night when the streets are empty. We are the only ones around in any direction. After eight months living out this way, I should know by now that this is what happens when you head toward the ocean, but I still hunch my shoulders, pull my denim jacket closer, and suck in my breath against the assault of a million moisture drops on wind. My quiet in the cold does not go unnoticed, as Andrew reaches out to touch my shoulder.

I think he's going to put his arm around mine, draw me into his masculine warmth in the way men like to pretend that they can, and I shrink away from it when I see it coming toward me in my peripheral. I'm not ready for that. It's too much, and I find myself wishing he would just go back to asking me those saccharine questions again, inject our friendship with falsities about why I live here and why he lives here and why any of us decided that this strange bay was a good place to house the book collections that make up their lives, giving me a way to avoid the truth. A way out. Without one in this moment, his touch seems more intrusively intimate than any of those questions that beg real answers – answers I never want to give – and my rapidly pumping heartbeats beg him to stop.

But this isn't what happens. Not at all. Instead he pinches the denim of my jacket in his fingers and gently tugs it back, forcing my shoulders to release their downward hunch and rise up, letting the fabric slip down a little, pulling my hands from their pockets where they can swing freely by my hips.

"You need to get your sea-lungs." His voice carries well in the semi-darkness of Fulton Street and comes out clear like the USF steeple bells we just trekked past.

"What?" I ask, confused.

"Your sea-lungs. The air in San Francisco isn't really that cold. It just feels cold when you try to block it out. If you stop resisting it, your body will adjust, and you'll feel that it's not really all that cold at all. That's your sea-lungs working."

He goes on to explain how I can get them for myself, how I can tap into that ability to make my mind warm up to the raw cold that seems impossible to escape on most days. Shoulders back, breathe in deeply — no, not necessarily deeply, just fully. It's really more of a confidence thing. Yes, that's it, just accept the cold into them, let it all in… He talks me through it.

And he's right. Suddenly, I'm not so cold any more. I still have to force my shoulders back against their instinct to hunch forward into fortress mode but I can feel the difference already. I imagine myself walking all around San Francisco this way, no longer afraid to feel the cold and frustrated that I can't just make it go away.

Andrew stays the night, and lingers for a bit in the morning. Sometime around dawn, he looks over and tells me I'm beautiful. I believe him, partly, and get up to grab us a glass of water, even though I know he'll probably get back together with his girlfriend in a few days or weeks.

When the sun starts pouring in through my half-closed blinds, bringing with it the noisy laughter of the children who live in the apartment below me as they chase each other around their grandmother's overgrown garden, he decides it's time for him to go. He has to finish a script, and I need a few hours to myself before I have to be back at the bar, pouring beers and answering questions.

"Elena Ferrante." I hear Andrew roll her name around in his

mouth a bit. I'm in the kitchen where I'm putting away the wine bottles we opened a few hours before, and wiping up a red spill I vaguely remember us laughing over. "I've heard the name," he says, "but I haven't read anything of hers yet. Is she any good?"

I had left the book on my dresser after finishing it weeks ago. Standing there, sink water running, Kay and Em pop into my mind, paralyzing it for a few seconds. I've been meaning to text them, to let them know I finally finished the book, to ask where in the world they are. But I haven't been able to bring myself to do it yet; it's almost as though I'm scared to bridge that distance after so many months of silence, worried that they'll tell me they aren't coming back after all, and in the back of my mind wondering nervously if they ever existed at all or if I just made them up completely out of desperation to find a community for myself so far from the one I was born into. That's how far away they feel. I left the book sitting there to remind myself, because putting it away on the shelf would be like putting them away almost.

"Yes, it's pretty good. A friend gave it to me. If you want, you can borrow it." It was actually amazing, which is why it took me so long to read. I kept crying at every particularly vivid paragraph, and so could never bring it with me on the bus or any other public place where you have to sit and wait and distract yourself.

"Yeah, I'd like that," he replies. I step back through the doorway and watch as he slips the book into his backpack before slinging it over his now-dressed shoulder and sighing briskly in a way that indicates he's just about ready to head out now, to put an end to our night together.

Downstairs, I open the door for him to walk out, which he does, after a brief obligatory kiss. When he moves out of the frame, I squint as the sun washes over the doorway, surprising me, so opposite of the cool darkness behind me in my apartment. It's both late enough and early enough that I don't need my new sea-lungs yet to tolerate it. In fact, it's kind of nice.

Turning away to go back inside, I catch sight of a colorful square poking out from our rusty gray mailbox, waving at me almost. I usually ignore the mail and let my roommates deal with it, but this one begged me to pick it up. A postcard. From the Grand Canyon. The front is a mix of purples and reds and oranges, depicting a sunrise over craggy rocks. Flipping it over, I scan to the bottom where I make out Kay's name from behind an ink-smudge, exactly what I was hoping to find there. My eyes zero in on the third to last line, nestled in the middle, holding the words I had been praying to see for months.

"On our way home now. Taking the long route, up towards Utah, but we'll definitely be back!"

Diamond Dave

E. Hagan

In retrospect, it is sweetly poignant to be reading the *Slingshot* newspaper this Sunday, stumbling upon it in a kiosk while tracing the Embarcadero. Their pocket-size planner, found in an anarchist bookstore in North Carolina, first pricked my ears to Berkeley in January. Reading activist anniversaries on demarcated days unearthed nostalgia for young adulthood, when I was captivated by the Trumbullplex collective in Detroit and engaged in subtle disruption in college, read *Adbusters*, and considered myself a socialist. Do people still do those things?

Fast forward a year and here I am enjoying seaside sun rays on my back, ostensibly waiting for something but really just absorbing the air, the sounds of busy people in a busy city. I sense a figure move past but don't file it away, my reading relegates the perception to the periphery. A short while later a voice – "Excuse me, maybe you can help me?" – I recognize the same presence beside me. I look up, and a small man, aged but not old, is looking down at me.

"I heard there is a procession on Market. Do you know about it?"

Well, I actually can help this person. Or at least I know what he is talking about. "A friend told me there is a protest starting at 3 at 555 California. I'm about to go over."

And thus begins my acquaintance with Diamond Dave.

"I had a feeling you were a kindred spirit. What are you reading?"

I show him the newspaper. This launches him into gently excited remembrances of his involvement with these and those guys for years, and Occupy Oakland and Bob Dylan and whatnot.

He tells me his age and date of birth several times, but it changes, I think, and he is suddenly hard to understand. It was recently his birthday, in any case. There was a celebration at Adobe Books. I know Adobe; I am blessed to live blocks away from Bookstore Row on 24th. I can certainly imagine Diamond Dave being a neighborhood character, and I can imagine them having a party for him, too.

He is perhaps shorter than shortish me, and has a few long blond dreadlocks down his back. When he lifts his hat his hair underneath is mostly gray, making me wonder how old those dreads are. He has a thick reddish, grayish, blondish beard slightly stained around the mouth. His face is deeply lined with sun/smile/smoking wrinkles and he has kind blue eyes. Eyes that really look. At one point, he said something, maybe quoted one of his poems, and I looked at him, and he said with a tone of wonder, "Look at you, looking at me, looking at you."

Often we don't trust ourselves, or dismiss instinctual reactions as irrelevant, but as he remarked on the present moment I was struck with the sense of something passed between us. Getting to know someone without many words. Or the words are more vessels for tone; he could have been humming his words to me, and I could've been humming back, and still we would gain a sense of connection and understanding.

He sits down facing me, legs crossed on the concrete bench with inspiringly age-defiant dexterity. Above a worn white sneaker, he pulls up the leg of his pant revealing a tattoo of a man riding a rocket. I recognize the *Dr. Strangelove* reference but ask, "Who's the guy?"

"It's me!"

And indeed it is. "Why is he wearing a sombrero?"

"Place here gave out free burritos for life if you got this tattoo; it's closed now," he says, mostly with satisfaction of his earnings. He added an anarchy circle-A to the drumhead of the missile for a personal touch.

We chat some more and as 3 p.m. nears, head off down Market together. Nothing appears to be going on at California, so we continue toward Market and Powell, and another hint of a gathering. Slowly we make our way down the sidewalk, passed by every other walker and vehicle on the street: it is surreal and lovely to be the slowest moving thing of a certain size in an environment.

Diamond Dave, a good talker and a good listener, quickly gets out of me that I moved here six months ago but am thinking about leaving; I haven't found the exploring, artistic, alternative folks I've been looking for. But now here is this man, a glimpse into communities existing undiscovered. I want to hear more stories of his history, the Occupiers, people he lives with by the flea market with the buses. I want to hear personally from the other side, those who do not toe the line, those who reject the story of success and normalcy no matter how comfortable it is. Those who lived it, are living it. He is giving me hope in this little walk from here to there.

"Isn't it something that I picked you out?" he keeps wondering aloud.

I've been marveling about that, too. How did that happen?

"Well," said Diamond Dave, "it was your energy. I'm old, I

could just sense it."

Which most people would dismiss, but really, I was sitting there head down, paper hidden as it was lying flat, not moving or speaking. I didn't notice him approach anyone else, he just came right up to me. I was open to him, maybe in need of something like this, and, bop, here he is.

It is time for me to go to work, and I have to pick up the pace, so I leave him a block from Powell.

"I hope there turns out to be a procession for you," I tell him.

"It doesn't matter," he responds. "We had this, our own procession."

I agree, and as I leave his world for my own, I am overcome by an unexpected sense of loss. I miss him already.

On the Way to Daly City

Peter Case

It was winter in San Francisco, late 1973. I'd been surviving with my guitar, living and playing on the street for most of the year. Joey the trumpet player was in our orbit now. He was from Brooklyn, had once played in some big Broadway musicals before coming West to get clean, to get away from the New York drug scene. He'd told us about his drug habit; he'd gotten deep into heroin, regularly tying off and fixing up with the rest of the horn section in the orchestra pit during the Broadway run of *Hello Dolly* while the conductor stood watch, looking out at the packed theater.

I loved hearing that story. Now he was out here with us, playing the streets in San Francisco and collecting ATD—"Aid for the Totally Dependent," known by everyone as "crazy pay" —which kept him in a house he shared in Daly City. ATD was a legendary California program. If you were certified nuts, ATD would pay your bills for the rest of your life. Most of us only dreamt about it but Joey had it. He was slick, really putting one over on them with his 'crazy' act, and every month when the check came in, Joey cashed it and went on an insane binge.

Joey was short, stocky, and bald. He dressed in brand new, oversized blue jeans that hung halfway down his ass. The cuffs were rolled up, and he stomped around in big black cop shoes, a black leather multi-zippered motorcycle jacket, and mirrored aviator shades, carrying a trumpet case in one hand and a black briefcase in the other where he kept his pistol, a black .38. I knew it was in there 'cause I saw him pull the gun once on a bagpipes player.

He was always exasperated, on the edge of flipping out, angry at the world, but the horn was his reason for living and he was pretty good when he wasn't too fucked up to play. He played straight New York commercial jazz.

One day, in a coffee house we'd ducked into to get out of the weather, Joey got up and performed "Theme From Exodus" on the piano for me and some guys. It sounded like shit. Digging his hammer-handed phrasing, seeing his hostile grimace behind the shades and his massacre of the grand melody, we fell out laughing. "Exodus" was his only number on the piano, but an exodus was the response it got from the rest of the audience.

I'd been out alone all day, was giving it one more try, busking on Beach Street in the cold early twilight, playing as a group of tourists passed me on the sidewalk like I was standing still. I couldn't bear anymore and was about to pack it up when I saw Joey coming up the street from the direction of The Cannery. He spotted me and headed straight over.

"Hey, Peter, man! I thought I'd find one of you guys out here. Whatchya doin'? This town ain't happenin'. It's dead, man! For losers. I wish I was in New York, I'm tellin' ya. Where's Danny, anyhow? Feldman is gettin' me some more work doin' commercials, and it beats this bullshit, man. Hey, let's play one, whaddaya say?"

He pulled out the horn, adjusted the mouthpiece, put it up to his lips, puckered up, and blew a hideous rasping, broken, descending squawk of a trumpet blast. We plowed our way through "Tea for Two," "Kansas City Blues," and gave up halfway into "Hello Dolly." It was pure musical pain and even with the added head-turning volume of the trumpet, no one cared. No money was ending up in the basket.

"This is nowhere, Case. C'mon, let's go over to the Haven. I need ya to drive me, man! I can't drive, I got my ATD check today...."

"Uh-huh."

"C'mon, man! I'll buy you some soup," he urged. "Then you can drive me home. I got room at my place. You can crash there tonight."

He pulled a little bottle out of his leather jacket, poured a few pills into his fist, then with a rapid motion tossed them into his mouth and choked 'em down without water. "It's my medicine, I gotta take it. Don' look at me like that," he said, and we set off to search for his car. We couldn't find the car and Joey was cursing. He figured it'd been stolen, and he was gonna kill whoever took it. He began to think his friend, the saxophone player Feldman, might be responsible.

"That motherfucker! He's a thief, Case. Can ya believe this shit? I go out of my way to help the guy, and he rips me off!"

I knew that Joey was lucky Feldman was even speaking to him after the outrages that had gone down the week before, but I said nothing. After spending thirty minutes wandering up and down Beach Street, we finally found the car—a little green late model VW—parked where he had left it, at a 45° angle to the curb. It had a parking ticket on the windshield, which he swore at, grabbed, and tossed in with the other junk in his briefcase.

We climbed in and headed cross town, with Joey lambasting me all the way with cursed directions, driving advice, and his psycho-social commentary. He'd lay back in the passenger seat, briefcase open on his lap, while official-looking papers fell out onto the floor. He kept wiping his hand over his face, sputtering, and knocking off his own glasses.

"Someday you'll learn, Case. If you wanna be a winner, you gotta act like a winner! Dress like a winner, do the things a winner would do."

Every so often, he'd go silent, then he'd lurch up in his seat, turn my way, and do a big double take, like he was noticing me there for the first time. We got over to the Haven, at California and Polk, and I parked. Joey took ten minutes getting out of the car, arranging things in the briefcase, putting them in, taking them out, switching his shades for black horn-rimmed glasses. Some of the papers fell out of the open car door and scattered in the street. "Oh, my prescriptions! Peter, help me! Pick those up before they blow away!"

I ran and chased the scraps from the gutter, finally caught them all, and brought them back. I handed them to Joey, who didn't say a word but became intent on stuffing them back into the pockets of his briefcase. Finally, we left the car and walked toward the restaurant.

The Haven, open 24 hours, was where the all-night people congregated for their avocado and sprouts on wheat bread, their healthy soups, Age of Aquarius salads, and strong coffee—as well as their speed, pot, Quaaludes, and heroin. The place was a combination of low rent health food restaurant and mystical whorehouse. It was dark inside, with the indirect lighting turned way down, and you could sit in the big leather booths till dawn if you wanted. No one seemed to care what you did, as long as you ordered something. The jukebox blared "My Guy," "Living for the City," "Let's Stay Together" constantly. The clientele was mostly gay men in their twenties, glittered rockers, drugsters, and nocturnal outlaws. From midnight to six a posse gathered out front in leather jackets and platform shoes, eye shadow and lipstick, chain-smoking, looking up and down the street, watching out for cops, waiting for the deal to go down. I found this place on my second day in California.

Joey staggered on the way in and collided with a skinny rock and roll kid by the door. The kid snapped, "Watch where you're going, Kojak!" but Joey didn't seem to notice and stumbled on past the cordon-rouge into the service line. The omelet traffic moved slowly, while Joey looked for his wallet, which he seemed to have misplaced.

"Case, that kid by the door, he kiped my billfold! Sonofabitch is a pickpocket!"

I looked up and saw the kid still standing by the door, his back to us, talking to someone with a beehive hairdo and plastic raincoat.

The jukebox was playing "Just Like Tom Thumb's Blues." I looked down and saw Joey's wallet, looking like a little dark turd on the floor, a few feet behind us. I went back and picked it up, then stepped forward and handed it to Joey, who was still frantically patting himself down. When he saw the wallet he immediately seized up, then grabbed it out of my hand and reared back.

"YOU! How did you get this? You crooked motherfucker! You stole my wallet? Don't fuck with me, Case!"

As he spoke, his eyes were focused on a spot in the middle of my forehead. Every few seconds they'd dart a quick look down into mine, meeting my glance for the tiniest of moments, than shifting back up to my forehead again.

"Easy, Joey! It was lying on the fucking floor where you dropped it. Maybe you should try and pay attention to what you're doing!"

He glowered at me, pretending he wasn't sure what to believe. Having a hard time focusing, he was looking at everything twice, and beads of sweat began forming on his upper lip. The line moved forward, and soon we were standing by the cauldrons of hot, steaming soups, several big black pots of 'em on the other side of the glass sneeze guard: minestrone, corn chowder, lobster, and French onion.

"What will you have?" asked the server, but Joey couldn't tell; he needed to make a closer inspection, so he bent over at the waist and reached his head under the glass and over the soups, to get a real good look. His glasses steamed up, then fell off, and landed—plop—in the Lobster bisque, floating on the simmering pink surface for a moment, before they sank in and vanished. Fucking Joey!

He jumped forward and reached his arms into the pot. The server was shouting, the bouncers were on us, dragging us to the door, and pushing us out. Joey was loudly complaining the whole way, "I want my glasses!" His shirt was splashed with soup stains, and his forearms were dripping with reddish viscous glop.

We finally got Joey's spectacles back. They were tossed out the door but not before Joey made a promise to kill the night manager if he ever saw him again. "I'll shoot you, you dirty fop!"

"Shoot yourself!" said the man, and we were back on the street.

The freeway south of the City was fogged in, nearly dead, as Joey's green Bug hurtled through the orange and grey striped light. Joey had curled up sideways in the passenger seat facing the door, nearly knocked out, mumbling curses and complaints as I drove. The world seemed far away, sort of stuffed, like I was watching it in a diorama. The radio was tuned to cheap jazz, and it sounded strange—kind of muffled, out of tune—and, in fact, everything seemed a little bit wrong, like God had come down and moved the furniture while we weren't looking.

We didn't eat after being bounced from The Haven. I was hungry but I figured the best thing to do was to get the first trumpet here off the street before the window of stoned opportunity slammed shut and we became really stranded. We just had to get to his pad in Daly City. I was tired I felt kind of sick myself.

We were about halfway there when the car started to blow it: wheezing, slowing, starting up again. We'd lose power for a second, the lights would dim and the engine choke, then it began to cough, shake, sputter, race, and whine. I didn't know what was wrong but I backed off the gas pedal then jammed it down hard, and after a second's delay, the car blasted something loud out of its backend, hesitated, lurched ahead, then recovered and took off. Everything seemed fine.

A moment later, the engine died completely, and I had to roll onto the shoulder, where we slowed to a halt. We sat there on the side of the road in the dark, me just staring straight ahead, and Joey now facing me. Everything was quiet except for the whoosh and fade of a passing car.

Joey began to rave. "What'd you do to my car, Case? You killed it. Can't you do anything? Man, I never should have let you drive! Where'd you grow up? Didn't anyone ever show you how to operate a car? I'm ready for Napa! I belong in there, for trusting somebody like you."

I was trying to start the car again but the engine wouldn't turn over. I tried again and again, but it just wouldn't make it, and at last I realized I was running the battery down. The car sounded desperate, like a tuberculosis victim trying to clear their throat, unable to breathe. I tried one last time, and it almost caught on, but after that it was never close.

Joey finally shut his mouth and leaned back in his seat, eyes toward the ceiling. He'd gone still and silent, maybe contemplating the seven stages of grief. I was trying to think of something, anything, 'cause until I did, I knew we'd be sitting there.

Who knew what would happen if the cops should stop and come across him in this state? They wouldn't be amused to find his gun, I knew that for starters. We had to get out of there, asap. If Joey could still walk I'd have suggested to just trundle off and abandon the car until we found somebody with jumper cables, but one look at Joey told me he wasn't walking nowhere. Whatever he'd taken outside the Haven as we left, well, it was good, and it had kicked in nice.

"Now listen, Joey, there's only one thing to do. I want you to pull yourself together, get out of the car, and come over here, sit in the driver's seat, and steer. I'm gonna get in back and push, get it started down the grade here. Once it gets going fast enough, all you gotta do is let out the clutch and it'll start, then just feed it a little gas, pull off to the side of the road, and let me catch up. Then I'll drive again, okay?"

That was okay with him, so I pulled on the parking brake and opened my door. I looked over and watched as Joey opened his door, took a first step out, and disappeared from view. He'd vanished right in front of my eyes. I sat there blinking for a second, dumbfounded and scared, then I got out of the car and ran around the back, over to his side, calling his name but he was nowhere in sight. What the hell?

"Helllllp! Peter! Hellllp!"

I looked over the side of the freeway embankment, way down over the steep slope of the gravel, jade plants, and dirt, and spied him—thirty feet down, the top of his head barely visible, floating like a little moon in the dark. He was moaning. "Help me! Help me, Peter!"

Fucking Joey! I scrambled and slid down the embankment, nearly losing my balance. When I got down there, I found him lying on his back, completely calm now, staring up at the sky and not moving. His eyes shifted toward me.

"I fell," he said.

I started trying to help him up the steep slope, and it was nearly too much. Tugging at his arms, shoving him, I felt his dead weight, smelled his perspiration and the stale whiff of his breath. We were covered in dirt; my knees and elbows were scraped and sore, both of us breathing like we were drowning, and now it was my turn to curse him. "C'mon, Joey! You fuckin' pig, you're not even trying! C'mon, motherfucker! Get it together!"

"I'm gonna kill you, Peter!"

"You ain't killing nobody, fucker! You can't even walk! Get your feet under you and push!"

With a superhuman effort, and after what seemed like eons, we made it to the top. But then, somehow I lost my balance and Joey loosed his grip, and he tumbled and slid all the way back to the bottom again.

Oh no! Time froze. We struggled in Purgatory, going on Hell. Finally, as I'd nearly lost my will to survive and was considering just stalking off and leaving him out there for the buzzards and the California Highway Patrol, we made it to the top somehow onto the level freeway shoulder, and I got him into the driver's seat. We were ready to go.

"You know what to do," I said. Then I got in back and pushed as hard as I could. The car wouldn't budge.

I yelled, "Joey! Take off the fucking brake!"

He released the brake. I got it going down the slight incline, slowly at first, then faster and faster. It picked up speed, but with me still pushing behind. Joey started to veer out into the highway, but just then a semi pulled up through the fog, nearly on top of us. "Joey! Argghhhh! Keep to the right!"

He steered it back over to the right, but now he was going too fast for me to keep up. I ran after him as he pulled away, gaining speed down the hill. "Start it, Joey! Start it now!"

I stopped running, dropped back, and watched as the green VW swerved down the hill, silently coasting, rolling off into the distance.

He made it onto the next exit off the road, and I could barely see him now. He was about a quarter mile away, still not starting the car, but just letting it roll down, then up, up, taking the rise, slower and slower, at last coming to a halt right there where the exit ramp started to bend, way up there 'neath the distant haloed streetlights.

Finally it stopped right in the middle of the road.

The taillights were on, everything was silent, Joey was just sitting there with his foot on the brake. I ran to catch up. My heart was pounding but I kept running. The car was motionless, and as I got within about twenty feet, Joey opened the door, and stepped out. He was standing there real cynical, pissed off because I was such a moron, just looking at me, shaking his head, his arms up over the open door, when the car started to roll slowly, backward down the grade. The door knocked him down. He fell to the pavement, and just as I got even with the car, the front left tire rolled over his foot.

I jumped into the car, stood on the brake, and stopped it. I put it into gear, put on the emergency brake, and got out. Joey was lying on his back, staring at the sky with the most extremely exasperated expression that I'd ever seen on anyone, anywhere.

He was kind of playing it for laughs. I helped him off the ground and into the passenger seat, and then I got behind the wheel again. I tried the starter, just out of habit, or desperation, sort of an automotive Hail Mary, and the engine started right up immediately, running fine, and we drove over to his place in Daly City.

The pad was perfectly middle class with doilies and knickknacks. Pillows were spruced up on the couch; it was very clean. Home Sweet Home plaques, a real Norman Rockwell kind of scene. There was a note on the kitchen counter from Joey's roommate saying he'd left town for a while.

Joey told me he was gonna stay up doing something, a high midnight rummaging he needed to do, but I told him I had to crash, and he offered me the roommate's bedroom, saying, "Make yourself at home."

Fine. I went in there and sat on the bed. It was an odd feeling, after spending a couple of years sleeping in blanket rolls and sleeping bags, to actually be in a bed between sheets. It felt nice but kind of weird. I turned out the lights and felt my way in the dark. The pillows were gigantic and seemed to glow in the dark. I nuzzled between them like they were two huge breasts, and sailed away into oblivion.

About the Writers

Dee Allen. is an African-Italian performance poet currently based in Oakland, California. Active on the creative writing and spoken word tips since the early '90s, he's the author of three books, *Boneyard, Unwritten Law,* and most recently *Stormwater,* and appears in 12 anthologies including *Poets 11: 2014, Feather Floating On The Water,* and the first four Revolutionary Poets Brigade books including *Rise,* among other titles. He is working on a fourth book.

Jorge Tetl Argueta is an award-winning author of picture books and poetry for young children. He is also the founder of La Biblioteca de los Sueños/Library of Dreams in El Salvador. He has won the International Latino Book Award, the Américas Book Award, the NAPPA Gold Award, the Independent Publisher Book Award for Multicultural Fiction for Juveniles, and the Lee Bennet Poetry Award. His books have also been named to the Américas Award Commended List, the USBBY Outstanding International Books

Honor List, Kirkus Reviews Best Children's Books, and the Cooperative Children's Book Center Choices. A native Salvadoran and Pipil-Nahua Indian, Jorge spent much of his life in rural El Salvador. He now lives in San Francisco, California, where he is Poet Laureate of the San Francisco Public Libraries.

Peter Case moved to San Francisco at age 18. A founding member of The Nerves and leader of The Plimsouls, he is a singer-songwriter, performer, and producer with 13 solo albums to his credit, including his self-titled T Bone Burnett-produced debut, the Grammy-nominated *Let Us Now Praise Sleepy John,* and *HWY 62.* He is also the author of a memoir, *As Far As You Can Get Without A Passport* (Evermore Books). After thirty years of LA living, he has returned to San Francisco.

Patsy Creedy has lived and worked in San Francisco for nearly thirty years. She has always loved poetry but has branched out into creative non-fiction and plain ole fiction. She recently completed an MA in creative writing, and now is pursuing an MFA at SF State. She works as a nurse, helping women deliver their babies. She has raised two tall children, and is an avid surfer.

Kelly Dessaint drives a San Francisco taxi and writes a weekly column about his misadventures in the city streets for the *SF Examiner.* An LA native exiled in Oakland with his wife and daughter, he is a veteran of the small press, the author of the novel *A Masque of Infamy* and currently publishes the personal narrative zine *Piltdownlad.* While he pledges allegiance to no baseball team, if he did, it would be the Giants.

Stefanie Doucette has finally found a home for herself in San Francisco, where she lives with two roommates and an impressively large plant collection. Born in Boston, MA and raised on a strong diet of feminism and early American ghostlore, she has a BA from the University of Vermont, and writes for *The Bold Italic* when not serving people beer.

Lynell George is a Los Angeles-based journalist, essayist and photographer. She has written for KCET's *Artbound, Los Angeles Times,* the *LA Weekly,* and she taught journalism at Loyola Marymount University. She is the author of *No Crystal Stair: African Americans in the City of Angels* (Verso/Doubleday).

John Goins, author of *A Portrait in the Tenderloin* and *The Coptic Cross,* was born in the southeast section of Washington, DC. He has worked as a dishwasher, library clerk, gardener, English teacher in Istanbul, telephone solicitor, phlebotomist and lab assistant. He also wrote briefly for the *Central City Extra,* a monthly newspaper for the Civic Center, Tenderloin, and Sixth Street Corridor. He lives and writes in San Francisco where he has resided, for the most part, since 1985. He published *A Portrait in the Tenderloin,* featuring reporter Bill Haywood, with Ithuriel's Spear in 2013.

E. Hagan is a sailboat powered by winds mysterious even to herself. A native Michigander, travels have taken her from Tibet to Appalachia, but she feels at home for the first time on the California coast. Currently tucked away under a zen mountain, E. earns her keep as a gardener on borrowed valley land. She is interested in exploring possibilities of the dream world, the symbolism of rocks and stars, how to hear an ancient story, the power of ritual and disengaging from social power structures. This is her first publication.

Michael Koch is a poet, translator, visual artist, and amateur percussionist whose Jamaican/Slavic roots only partly explain his passion for syncopation and absurdity. His published work has appeared in, among others, *Beatitude, Hanging Loose, Toad Suck Review, River Styx, Five Fingers Review, Nicotine Soup, Durak,* and *Third Rail.* His translations also appear in the City Lights anthology of contemporary Cuban poetry, *Island of My Hunger,* and the City Lights collection of contemporary Mexican poetry, *Light from a Nearby Window.*

Raluca Ioanid was born in communist Romania and raised in capitalist New York City. By day, she is a Family Nurse Practitioner at a community health center in Fruitvale, Oakland. By night, she is a traveling, trapeze flying, writer of stories. Her work has appeared in *The Sun, Riverbabble,* and *So To Speak.*

Sylvia J. Martínez is a writer and adult school ESL teacher. Her work has appeared in *In Media Res: Stories from the In-Between* (WriteSpace)*, the East Bay Review, Cipactli, Word Riot, Tattoo Highway,* and the *San Francisco Examiner,* among others. She earned her MFA from San Francisco State and is working on her first collection of stories. She lives in the SF Bay Area with her husband, two teenage children, and dog.

Alvin Orloff is the author of three whimsical queer novels: *I Married an Earthling, Gutter Boys,* and *Why Aren't You Smiling?* and co-author of *The Unsinkable Bambi Lake,* a transgender showbiz memoir. He currently works at Dog Eared Books Castro, a quaint neighborhood bookstore, and continues to write, his latest project being a book about crazy, slutty club kids during the height of the AIDS crisis. He worries that life is passing him by, so if you invite him to do something (contribute to your magazine, appear in your movie, lecture your Creative Writing class, go out for drinks, what have you) the answer will almost certainly be "yes."

Tony Robles is a born and raised San Franciscan poet and children's author. Like his uncle, the late Manilatown and I-Hotel poet Al Robles, he is referred to as "The People's Poet." Author of the poetry/short story collection *Cool Don't Live Here No More: A Letter to San Francisco* and the forthcoming *Fingerprints of a Hunger Strike* (Ithuriel's Spear Press), he was nominated for a Pushcart Prize by Mythium Journal for his short story, "In My Country". He has been a recipient of the San Francisco Arts Commission Individual Artist Grant.

Alice Elizabeth Rogoff has MAs in Creative Writing and Drama from San Francisco State University, and a BA in Anthropology from Grinnell College. She has been published in *Caveat Lector, Pudding Magazine, Borderlands,* and *Black Maria.* She has two books of poetry, *Mural* and *Barge Wood.* She has received an Individual Cultural Equity Commission from the San Francisco Arts Commission.

Broke-Ass Stuart aka **Stuart Schuffman** is a TV host, a travel writer, a poet, a *San Francisco Examiner* columnist, a former mayoral candidate, and a motherfucking hustler.

Shizue Seigel is a third-generation Japanese American writer and visual artist who has lived in San Francisco since 1958. She loves the city's ever-changing diversity, but misses the Fillmore, the old Mission, and Japantown, fog and foghorns, working docks, the Belt Line. Her books include *In Good Conscience: Supporting Japanese Americans during the Internment, Century of Change: the Memoirs of Nellie Nakamura, Distillations: Meditations on the Japanese American Experience,* and *Standing Strong: Fillmore and Japantown.* Her poetry and prose have been published in numerous anthologies and journals, and recognized by the National League of American PEN Women. Her work is archived at UC Santa Barbara's California Ethnic and Multicultural Archives, and solo exhibitions of her visual art include *Laramie: Mapping Myths and Realities, Double Vision: A Celebration of Hybridity, and Ephemeral Allure; Eternal Struggle* at UC Santa Barbara. Her latest project, *Endangered Species,* is forthcoming.

Kim Shuck is a jester, activist, bead artist, poet, and San Franciscan. Shuck has authored three full-length books and one chapbook, including her latest, *Clouds Running In* (Taurean Horn Press). In 2017, she was named Poet Laureate of San Francisco.

Don Skiles is the author of *Miss America and Other Stories, The James Dean Jacket Story,* and the novel *Football.* His collection of short fiction, *Rain After Midnight* was published in 2017 by Pelekinesis Press. He lives in San Francisco.

Anna Maria Smith is a native San Franciscan now living in Los Angeles, where she dreams of Muni buses, the San Francisco Giants, and the Golden Gate Bridge. She is the owner of ZiBoom, an international community for individuals over the age of 45. In her spare time, she is happily married to Sam and takes orders from four dogs.

Barbara Stauffacher Solomon is a Swiss-trained graphic designer with a masters degree in architecture. An award-winning landscape artist, she conceived the signage and supergraphics at The Sea Ranch, Ghirardelli Square, and the Ribbon of Light along the Embarcadero in San Francisco. Her books, *Green Architecture & The Agrarian Garden, Plays on a Page, Good Mourning California, Why?WhyNot?, UtopiaMyopia,* and *Super-Silly-Us* are pix and prose juxtaposed, each a series of drawings plus text, hand typeset and pasted up on 8-1/2 x 11 sheets of paper.

Denise Sullivan is a fourth generation San Franciscan who writes about music, arts and culture, and her hometown. She has lived in Atlanta, Los Angeles, and again in San Francisco, has contributed to dozens of newspapers, magazines, websites, and reference books,, and has published six titles , including *Keep on Pushing: Black Power Music From Blues to Hip Ho*p (Lawrence Hill Books/Chicago Review Press).

Norman Antonio Zelaya was born and raised in San Francisco. He has published stories in *ZYZZYVA, NY Tyrant, 14 Hills, Cipactli,* and *Apogee Journal,* among others, and was a 2015 *Zoetrope: All-Story* finalist. He is a founding member of Los Delicados, and has performed extensively throughout the US with them. Zelaya has appeared on stage, in film, and in the squared circle as luchador, Super Pulga. Currently, he lives and works in San Francisco's Mission District as a special education teacher. *Orlando & Other Stories* is his first published book.

Acknowledgments

The events that led to the publication of this collection took place over a 30-year period and culminated one night in the summer of 2016. Thanks to Jason Christopher Mull for overseeing the Writer-in-Residence program at Alley Cat Books and for encouraging me to read my work in progress. Thanks to Jennifer Joseph for attending the reading and inviting me to field the contributors and submissions to a San Francisco anthology. As a first-time editor, I am grateful to her for sharing her editorial expertise. Thanks to all of the writers who submitted their work for consideration, and to those included within these pages, without whom there would be no book. Thanks to my coworkers at the Modern Times Bookstore Collective, and to our friends at Dog Eared Books and Adobe Bookshop — the United Booksellers of San Francisco. The following people and organizations contributed in ways seen and unseen toward the completion of this project and I wish to thank them for their contributions: Calle 24 Arts and Cultural Assets Committee, Litquake, St. John Coltrane African Orthodox Church, San Francisco Poet Laureates Alejandro Murguía and Kim Shuck, Victor Krummenacher, Marilyn Roxie, Gail Meadows, and Peter Case.

Some of these works have previously appeared as noted below, in slightly different forms:

"A Tale of Three Cities," by Broke-Ass Stuart, was published as a column in the *San Francisco Examiner*

"Lago de Los Dolores," by Alvin Orloff, was published as a chapbook by Bent Boy Books

"Awful Sweet," by Denise Sullivan, was published as the title story in a chapbook by Alley Cat Books

"State of Being" by Lynell George, was published as a story by *Boom: A Journal of California*